"In the popular mind, fact and fiction about the Catholic priesthood do not simply exist side by side but feed on each other. We owe Ambrose Mong a debt of gratitude as he disentangles real-life stories and the imaginative world of novels. What emerges from Mong's profound analysis is the figure of the priest as a flesh-and-blood human person who, though a sinner, can become holy through suffering and God's love and mercy. The book is a must-read after the clergy sex-abuse scandal."
—PETER C. PHAN
Ignacio Ellacuria chair of Catholic social thought, Georgetown University

"Ambrose Mong's tales of priests in these pages never glorify the priesthood in a way that takes away their humanity. Whether in real life or in classic fiction, these are men who are larger than life, but always human, always struggling, always growing in their baptismal identity as sacraments of God's love in our world. In a church wracked with scandals of clerical abuse and continuing clericalism, this is a book of inspiration and hope."
—STEPHEN B. BEVANS
Louis J. Luzbetak, SVD, professor of mission and culture, emeritus,
Catholic Theological Union

"Priests come in all shapes and sizes. Whether factual or fictional, the priestly lives examined by Ambrose Mong provide a rich tapestry, shedding light on the complexities experienced to some degree by many priests, and the people they serve, as they face the challenges of authentic Christian living."
—PATRICIA MADIGAN
Dominican Centre for Interfaith Ministry, Education and Research, Australia

"Saints are not perfect people. They are people who know their need of God. In Ambrose Mong's fine book, modern novelists portray the interior lives of priests who have fought to keep alive the light of Christ in an often-dark world. Mong explores the remarkable commitment of priests and bishops in China, Japan, and San Salvador, using also the insights of fiction from Willa Cather, George Bernanos, and Graham Greene to illuminate the faith and courage of men, not perfect but extraordinary in their faith and love for suffering humanity."

—DAVID JASPER
Honorary professorial research fellow, University of Glasgow

# Treasure in Earthen Vessels

# Treasure in Earthen Vessels

### The Portrayal of Priests in Fact and Fiction

## AMBROSE MONG

CASCADE *Books* • Eugene, Oregon

Cascade Books
An Imprint of Wipf and Stock Publishers
199 W. 8th Ave., Suite 3
Eugene, OR 97401

www.wipfandstock.com

PAPERBACK ISBN: 979-8-3852-1575-1
HARDCOVER ISBN: 979-8-3852-1576-8
EBOOK ISBN: 979-8-3852-1577-5

*Cataloguing-in-Publication data:*

Names: Mong, Ambrose [author].

Title: Treasure in earthen vessels : the portrayal of priests in fact and fiction / Ambrose Mong.

Description: Eugene, OR: Cascade Books, 2025 | Includes bibliographical references and index.

Identifiers: ISBN 979-8-3852-1575-1 (paperback) | ISBN 979-8-3852-1576-8 (hardcover) | ISBN 979-8-3852-1577-5 (ebook)

Subjects: LCSH: Catholic Church—Clergy—Fiction. | Priests—Fiction. | Priesthood. | Clergy—Office. | Catholic Church—Clergy.

Classification: BX4794.16 M66 2025 (paperback) | BX4794.16 (ebook)

VERSION NUMBER 012425

For Ben Chang

## Thou Art a Priest Forever

To live in the midst of the world
without wishing its pleasures;
To be a member of each family,
yet belonging to none;
To share all suffering;
to penetrate all secrets;
To heal all wounds;
to go from men to God
and offer Him their prayers;
To return from God to men
to bring pardon and hope;
To have a heart of fire for Charity,
and a heart of bronze for Chastity
To teach and to pardon, console and bless always.
My God, what a life;
and it is yours,
O priest of Jesus Christ!

*Jean-Baptiste Henri Lacordaire, OP (1802–1861)*

# Contents

# Preface and Acknowledgments

In his *Letter to a Suffering Church*, Bishop Robert Barron describes the clerical sexual abuse as a "diabolical masterpiece." This scandal has completely undermined the church's credibility and crippled its mission to educate and help those in need. Countless lives, especially the most vulnerable, have been destroyed. According to Barron, this evil act is not just a result of human weakness, but a deliberate plan orchestrated by the devil, with the willing participation of the perpetrators. It is a devastating blow to the church and its members, a true "devil's masterpiece."

Throughout history, the church has been tainted by sin, scandal, and stupidity. St. Paul acknowledges the imperfections of the early Christian communities, comparing the grace of Christ to a treasure held in fragile clay jars (2 Cor 4:7). Despite these flaws, we choose to remain in the church because, like Peter, we say, "Lord, to whom shall we go? You have the words of eternal life" (John 6:68). In Jesus, we find salvation and the fulfillment of our deepest desires. While there are valid reasons to criticize the church, there is never a valid reason to abandon it. We may be shocked and upset by the corruption and misconduct of the clergy, but we must never turn away from God's grace.

Despite its failings, the church proclaims the message of God and the mystery of Christ's redemption. It is the body of Christ that can satisfy our heartfelt longings. Since the beginning, the Holy Spirit has been present in the church, breathing life into this mystical body. While we have witnessed the terrible corruption and sexual scandals within our church, we must not forget the examples of the saints and the priests who have been beacons of light in this dark period. In response to the media's almost totally negative portrayal of the Catholic church, I have endeavored to depict real-life clerics and fictional characters from various historical and cultural backgrounds to show that there are still good priests among us. In the conclusion, I have also shared my personal experience of one such priest.

Finally, I would like to thank Ben Chang for presenting me with a copy of Bishop Barron's work, which moved me to write this book. I am also very grateful to Kenzie Lau and Ellen McGill for their proofreading, editing, and valuable comments. Francis Chin, Brother Patrick Tierney FSC, and Father Brian Vale SSC have also been very supportive with their proofreading and suggestions. Any error that remains is, of course, my own.

Ambrose Mong
St. Joseph's Church
Central, Hong Kong

# Introduction

IN HISTORY AND IN literature, priests have often been portrayed as heroic figures battling evil or facing moral dilemmas. These depictions emphasize their unwavering faith and commitment even in the face of great personal sacrifice. In movies and novels, priests are often featured as flawed characters struggling to fulfill their religious duties. These portrayals aim to show priests as fallible human beings, facing their own challenges while remaining faithful to their calling.

Despite their shortcomings, priests are often lauded as devoted and virtuous, known for their dedication, faithfulness, and commitment to serving their communities. They are often described as compassionate, wise, and thoughtful individuals who provide spiritual guidance and support to their congregations.

Authors sometimes focus on the moral authority of clergy, particularly bishops who lead their flocks through challenging circumstances, such as during times of persecution. These clerics uphold the teachings of the church with integrity and loyalty.

Yet priests, like any human being, have their flaws and struggles, though their adversities provide profound lessons for us. This work aims to express and explain the personal doubts, temptations, and internal conflicts that priests face in fulfilling their duties. It strives to reveal the complexities and challenges encountered by priests who have dedicated their lives to caring for souls.

Portrayals of clergy often reflect the perspectives and biases of those presenting them and may not accurately represent the true complexity of the priests. Positive portrayals highlight their compassion, wisdom, and dedication to serving their communities, spotlighting them as moral guides offering spiritual guidance and support. The positive impact that priests have on the lives of individuals and communities has been well documented.

Recent years, however, have seen the media reporting scandals and controversies involving Catholic priests, including sexual and financial misconduct. These stories expose the dark side of the institution, with attempts to cover up wrongdoing in order to protect the church's reputation and maintain support from its followers at the expense of the victims. Sexual abuses by priests have occurred in various parts of the world, causing great harm to the victims. These incidents have rightfully sparked public outrage and demands for accountability.

While we cannot ignore these evil deeds, we must remember that these wayward clerics do not represent the entire priesthood. Negative portrayals have contributed to stereotypes and misconceptions about the Catholic priesthood, promoting a flawed and biased image. When critically examining such negative portrayals, it is even more necessary that we acknowledge the many priests who sincerely strive to live out their faith and vocation while serving the people of God.

The Catholic church has taken steps to address and prevent abuse within its ranks. Efforts have been made to implement safeguarding measures, improve transparency, and provide support to victims of abuse. However, the media often focuses on the institution's failures in addressing this crisis rather than on the serious attempts being made to rectify the situation.

Negative portrayals of Catholic priests exist in various forms. It is crucial, however, that we distinguish between the actions of a few individuals and the priesthood's overall character and commitment. With this in mind, I have written this work to depict priests in both factual and fictional scenarios throughout history, aiming to convey the complexity of each individual cleric as they try to fulfill their duties as shepherds of the flock.

The work comprises several chapters that focus on different aspects of religious figures and their journeys. Chapter 1 delves into the complexities and conflicts within the Catholic church of China, exemplified by the lives and actions of two bishops: Ignatius Kung and Aloysius Jin Luxian.

Chapter 2 explores the life of the Jesuit Pedro Arrupe, highlighting the stages in which he faced significant suffering that deepened his connection with God and people. His ideas and proposals remain relevant in tackling the challenges of our modern world.

Chapter 3 discusses the life and teachings of Archbishop Óscar Romero, who preached forgiveness and reconciliation in a nation torn by violence. Romero emphasized the importance of justice and truth in achieving lasting peace.

Chapter 4 analyses Willa Cather's rendering of Bishop Jean Latour in *Death Comes for the Archbishop*, tracing his transformation from an ambitious church leader to a compassionate priest who embraces local traditions and spirituality.

Chapter 5 focuses on the character development of the protagonist in George Bernanos's *The Diary of a Country Priest*. Through encounters with the rural community, the young priest evolves into a mature and compassionate pastor, finding grace and redemption through his struggles.

Chapter 6 examines the themes of faith, sin, and salvation in Graham Greene's *The Power and The Glory*, centering on the figure of the morally flawed priest. Despite persecution and personal failings, the priest's execution paradoxically represents the triumph of Christianity.

Chapter 7 delves into Shusaku Endo's novel *Silence* and the transformation of the protagonist, Rodrigues, as he grapples with the renunciation of his faith. Through humiliation and shame, he experiences a shift towards a more authentic and empathetic faith in the suffering of Jesus.

Each chapter contributes to a nuanced exploration of the challenges and growth experienced by these religious figures, shedding light on different aspects of their journeys. Priests are humans, but some of these individuals transcend adversity and life-threatening struggles to stay true to their mission and commitment.

# Chapter 1

# A Tale of Two Visionary Bishops in China

And it shall come to pass afterward, that I will pour out my Spirit upon all flesh; and your sons and your daughters shall prophesy, your old men shall dream dreams, your young men shall see visions: and also upon the servants and upon the handmaids in those days will I pour out my Spirit.

—Joel 2:28

I am a Roman Catholic Bishop. If I denounce the Holy Father, not only would I not be a Bishop, I would not even be a Catholic. You can cut off my head, but you can never take away my duties.

—Bishop Ignatius Kung Pin-mei

I am both a serpent and a dove. The government thinks I'm too close to the Vatican, and the Vatican thinks I'm too close to the government. I'm a slippery fish squashed between government control and Vatican demands.

—Bishop Aloysius Jin Luxian

Two MEN, EACH A spiritual giant in his own right, embodied the oft-quoted prophecy from the Book of Joel given above—Ignatius Kung Pin-Mei and Aloysius Jin Luxian, both bishops of Shanghai. The prophecy speaks of a time when God's Spirit will be poured out upon all people, and that this will lead to a renewed sense of prophecy, vision, and spiritual courage.

Since 1949 when the Red Army took over the whole of China, both Ignatius Kung and Aloysius Jin faced immense challenges serving the church and its flock in Shanghai and its vicinity. Both suffered long imprisonment, yet they never wavered in their faith that God's word will ultimately triumph. They continued to pray, to offer spiritual guidance to others, and to stand up for what they believed in. They were living examples of how God's Spirit can empower people to overcome adversity and to live out their faith in even the most difficult circumstances. Nonetheless, both differed in their personal responses to the threats and blandishments from the Chinese Communist Party.

## Face-Off with the Authorities

It was October 1, 1949. After a long bitter civil war, the Red Army under Chairman Mao Zedong finally drove out troops of the corrupt, inept Nationalist Government and proclaimed a People's Republic. Six days later, Ignatius Kung was appointed the first native bishop of Shanghai. But the new rulers were officially atheists, and it was decreed that the old gods worshipped by the Chinese population (at that time, around four hundred million people) must be crushed. The Communist Party's attitude was that religion was "the opiate of the masses," a temporary historical phenomenon that would disappear as society advanced. As for those citizens who were not sufficiently enlightened to share this view, they, together with their bishops, priests, monks, and religious teachers, had to be safely locked away. Chairman Mao and his ruling clique at the time described religion as being linked to "foreign cultural imperialism." Organized religious groups were persecuted across the board, with particular focus on Christians for their ties to foreign missionaries and the Vatican.

Ignatius Kung as the new bishop of Shanghai proved to be extraordinarily stubborn and became one of the earliest victims of this iron-fisted ideology. In 1951, the regime expelled the Papal Nuncio and severed diplomatic ties with the Holy See. More than a decade later, Chairman Mao launched the Cultural Revolution (1966–76) after perceiving enemies under the bed and everywhere else, including even among his own redder-than-red comrades. All religious activities, including those of the Catholic Church, were forbidden. Churches were closed; many priests and laity were arrested and imprisoned. During this period of persecution, the underground church emerged, with believers practicing in secret. Realizing that it was impossible to suppress the faith, the Communist government decided to divide the Catholic Church by establishing its own Chinese Catholic Patriotic Association in 1957, independent of Vatican control.

In view of this conflict and tension between the underground and official church, the appointment of bishops was considered the most contentious issue because it dealt with the leadership of the local churches, which both parties were determined to control. The Vatican naturally insisted that it had the right to appoint bishops through the Holy See headed by the pope. It stressed communion between the local churches and the universal church with the pope as the symbol of unity. Local church organizations could appoint bishops but only with the pope's approval.

Through the decades since 1949, the Communist regime has always viewed the Vatican as a foreign city-state. Hence, it does not want the Holy See to interfere with the affairs of the church in China. It associates the Catholic Church with the rapacious Western imperialist forces that humiliated China from the mid-nineteenth century until the Japanese invasion in 1931.

Thus the government sought to establish a so-called independent, self-managed church, which includes the selection and consecration of bishops approved by the Communist Party. This process violates the theological principle of catholicity and unity.

The complexity and conflict within the Catholic Church of China are personified by the careers and actions of two bishops, Ignatius Kung (1901–2000) and Aloysius Jin Luxian (1916–2013).[1]

## Staunch Catholic Origins

Born in born in Tangmuqiao Village in Chuansha County, Jiangsu Province, on August 2, 1901, Ignatius Kung came from a staunch Catholic family. He studied at Xuhui College (St. Ignatius High School) in Shanghai before entering the Xujiahui seminary in 1920. It was a diocesan seminary administered by French Jesuits, which taught philosophy, theology, and canon law. Kung completed his priestly studies in 1928, and after two years of pastoral work, Kung was ordained on May 28, 1930. His official duties and responsibilities included being student chaplain and headmaster of various schools in Songjiang and Shanghai.

Kung became the first native Chinese bishop of Shanghai when he was consecrated on October 7, 1949, seven days after Chairman Mao proclaimed the People's Republic. A faithful shepherd, Kung refused to renounce his fidelity to the Roman Catholic Church despite the life sentence meted out to him by the Chinese Communist Party. Kung stood by his clergy and was faithful for months before his arrest in 1955, despite offers of safe passage out of China. A man who inspired millions of Catholics, Kung fought hard for religious freedom and against human rights violations in the country.

As bishop of Shanghai, Kung became one of the most prominent critics of the Communist regime. In defiance of the government, he personally directed the Legion of Mary, a lay organization dedicated to the veneration of the Blessed Virgin Mary through good works. As a result, members of the Legion, many of them students, were arrested and sent to prison. In the midst of persecution, Kung declared 1952 the Marian Year in Shanghai. During that year, there was continuous recitation of the rosary. Armed

1. Some material in this chapter appeared in Mong, *Sino-Vatican Relations*, 128–35.

police were present in the church of Christ the King where Kung was leading a rosary. At the end of the recitation, Kung prayed, "Holy Mother, we do not ask you for a miracle. We do not beg you to stop the persecutions. But we beg you to support us who are very weak."[2]

Aware that he would soon be arrested, Kung trained many catechists to continue imparting the faith to future generations. The work of these catechists, their sacrifices and their deaths, contributed greatly to the growth of the underground church movement. A New Year youth rally held in 1953 proclaimed, "Bishop Kung, in darkness you light up our path. . . . You are the foundation rock of our Church in Shanghai."[3]

On September 8, 1955, Ignatius Kung was arrested along with Aloysius Jin and more than two hundred priests and lay leaders in Shanghai. Months later, Ignatius Kung was taken to a "struggle session" in a dog-racing stadium in Shanghai where he was forced to confess his "crimes" in front of thousands of people. Wearing pajamas and with his hands tied behind his back, Kung was pushed forward towards the microphone. He confessed, "Long live Christ the King, long live the pope." The crowd responded immediately, "Long live Christ the King, long live Bishop Kung!" Shocked, the security police quickly dragged Kung into their car. Brought to trial, he was sentenced to life in prison.

The night before the trial, the chief prosecutor asked if Kung was willing to lead the Chinese Catholic Patriotic Association, an organization controlled entirely by the Communist Party. Kung replied, "I am a Roman Catholic Bishop. If I denounce the Holy Father, not only would I not be a Bishop, I would not even be a Catholic. You can cut off my head, but you can never take away my duties."[4] For the next thirty years, he was behind bars spending long periods in isolation. Not allowed to have visitors from religious and human rights organizations or from officials of foreign states, Kung was also prevented from receiving visits from family

2. Cardinal Kung Foundation, "Biography."
3. Cardinal Kung Foundation, "Biography."
4. Cardinal Kung Foundation, "Biography."

and relatives, letters, and money to buy essential things, which were the rights of other prisoners.

With Kung in jail, the Chinese government named a Jesuit, Aloysius Zhang Jiashu (1893–1988), as bishop in 1960. Thus at that time in Shanghai, there was Kung, a legitimate bishop, in jail, and a puppet bishop, Zhang, in office. Zhang was never approved by Rome.[5]

Released in July 1985, but remaining under house arrest until January 6, 1988, Kung had his political rights restored by the Shanghai court. The court said Kung had "admitted his crime and showed repentance" and he would "abide by the law and pledge allegiance to his country."[6] There was no direct statement from Kung and the wording of the press releases was ambiguous. This suggests that it was the authorities, and not Kung, that relented. Perhaps by releasing him, the Chinese government hoped to have friendlier relations with the Vatican. Kung's suffering in prison was more of an embarrassment than a threat to the image of China as a world-class nation.

After his release Kung was permitted to attend a banquet organized by the government to welcome Cardinal Jaime Sin of Manila, who was on a friendship visit. During the dinner, Cardinal Sin invited each person to sing a song to celebrate the occasion. In the presence of Communist officials and bishops of the Patriotic Association, Kung sang in Latin, *Tu es Petrus et super hanc petram aedificabo Ecclesiam* ("You are Peter and upon this rock I will build my Church," Matt 16:18).[7]

After the banquet, Aloysius Jin, who was then the state-appointed bishop of Shanghai, rebuked Kung, "What are you trying to do? Showing your position?" Kung quietly answered, "It is not necessary to show my position. My position has never changed."[8] In spite of years of unimaginable suffering, isolation, and pain,

5. Mariani, "Four Catholic Bishops of Shanghai," 41.
6. "Witness of Bishop Gong," 23.
7. Cardinal Kung Foundation, "Biography."
8. Cardinal Kung Foundation, "Biography."

Cardinal Sin reported that this man of God never faltered in his love for the church and the pope.

During the visit of President Jiang Zemin to the United States in 1997, Kung petitioned Jiang to allow religious freedom in China: "I respectfully appeal to you, Mr. Chairman, to defend the rights of the Chinese citizens to true religious freedom, and to permit the Roman Catholics to maintain true religious freedom, and to permit the Roman Catholics to maintain religious communion with the Pope in order to keep the fullness of their faith. May China, under your able leadership, be internationally known as a country which has true religious freedom."[9] Obviously, religious freedom and the welfare of the Catholic Church in China was not a priority in Jiang's presidency.

Kung never ceased praying for those who had separated themselves from the pope and joined the Catholic Patriotic Association. Through the radio, he invited the Patriotic Association bishops to be in communion with Rome. Bishop Fulton Sheen said, "The West has its Mindszenty, but the East has its Kung. God is glorified in His saints."[10] Ignatius Kung died on March 12, 2000, at age ninety-eight.

## Counter-Revolutionary Crimes

> Ninety years is a lot of living, thirty years in Chinese Communist prisons is putting human nature to the test. Long periods of solitary confinement are surely a stressful experience. . . . Anyone living through such a heavy trial, just has to be made of sterner stuff.[11]

As mentioned, when the Chinese Catholics were persecuted, Ignatius Kung stayed with the faithful, comforting and strengthening them in the faith. He counselled them, "If we deny our faith, we will die and there will be no resurrection. If we stay faithful, we

9. Cardinal Kung Foundation, "Biography."
10. Cardinal Kung Foundation, "Biography."
11. Houle, "One of Christ's Heroes," 58.

7

will still die, but there will be resurrection."[12] After his arrest, Kung was subjected to harsh punishment and privations in prison. What were his crimes?

Bishop Kung was tried in Shanghai at the municipal court in March 1960 and was found guilty of counter-revolutionary and anti-government activities under the guise of religion, of collaborating with imperialists, and of betraying the motherland.[13] Sentenced to life imprisonment, Kung was stripped of all his political rights. It was understood by the Western world that the condemnation of Kung was due to his loyalty to the Holy See, which the Chinese authorities perceived as treason.

Another of Kung's stated offences was his withdrawal of support for China in the Korean War (1950–53), a position regarded as traitorous. China entered the Korean War in support of North Korea's invasion of the South. To mobilize support for the war, the Chinese government formed a new movement, the Resist America, Aid Korea Movement (RA-AK). Not to take part in this organization was considered treason. Many prominent priests, including Beda Chang (1905–51), a leading Jesuit educator in Shanghai, by forbidding Catholics to enlist in the army, were accused of sabotaging the war effort. Nearly one million Chinese, including Mao's son, died fighting in this pointless war. Thus Catholics who did not support the war effort was considered lackeys of the imperial powers.[14]

Years later, Kung confirmed that he was sentenced to life imprisonment for his refusal to sever ties with the Vatican and to hand over leadership as bishop of Shanghai and apostolic administrator of Suzhou and Nanjing to the Patriotic Association. That would mean giving the Communist Party complete control and spiritual authority over the Catholic Church in China.

During his years in prison, Kung said, "I prayed and I acted as the bishop of this city, sharing my people's sufferings. With God, time is never wasted." Pope John Paul II made him a cardinal as

12. John Paul II, "Chinese Cardinal Ignatius Kung Pin-mei Dies."
13. Catholic World Report, "Profile in Courage."
14. Mariani, *Church Militant*, 167.

"the expression of my heartfelt esteem, openness, and good will towards the great Chinese family." The Holy Father said Kung had "given witness by word and deed, through long suffering and trials, to what constitutes the very essence of life in the Church: participation in the divine life through the apostolic faith and evangelical love." The pope added that Kung's elevation to the College of Cardinals "is a tribute to your humble perseverance in this necessary communion with Peter."[15]

An article in a Hong Kong daily newspaper, *Chan Po*, reported, "Red China has sentenced Kung Pin-Mei for life. Logically speaking it should be a victory for the Chinese Communists. But I say definitely that the victory belongs to Bishop Kung Pin-Mei."[16] The reporter, a non-believer, observed that the bishop had great influence over the people, and this was what the Chinese Communists feared most. They arrested Kung only after they had failed to persuade him to denounce the Vatican as a collaborator with American imperialists. With his strong influence over the Catholic population, Kung's cooperation would be a great help to the Communist anti-religion movement, but the bishop stood firm in his refusal. Thus, after six years of persuasion, they gave up and punished him. But for a man of faith, it didn't matter: "Victory does not go to those who hold power and force, but to those who have faith."[17]

After the trial, Ignatius Kung was moved from prison to prison and finally ended up in the Ward Street Jail in Shanghai, where he stayed for twenty-nine years. While in prison, he was forbidden to celebrate Mass, read the Bible, or receive visitors. After his release in 1988, Kung admitted that he had used his fingers to recite the rosary. When in solitary confinement, the bishop would make the thirty-day Ignatian retreat every month. During the three decades that he spent in prison, he wrote prayers in Chinese, most of

---

15. John Paul II, "Chinese Cardinal Ignatius Kung Pin-mei Dies."

16. Quoted in DiGiovanni, *Ignatius*, 77.

17. Quoted in DiGiovanni, *Ignatius*, 80.

poor in rural areas, was murdered in 1977, Romero realized he had to take sides, but also to be prepared to forgive.

At the funeral mass for Fr. Rutilio Grande and the two companions who were killed, Romero preached that the church, inspired by love, is able to reject hatred:

> We want to tell you, murderous brothers, that we love you and that we ask of God repentance for your hearts, because the church is not able to hate, it has no enemies. Its only enemies are those who want to declare themselves so. But the church loves them: "Father forgive them, they know not what they do."[7]

Later Romero acknowledged that it had been the assassination of Rutilio Grande, his personal friend, that had motivated him to put into practice the teachings of Vatican II and the Latin American Bishops' conference at Medellín, calling for solidarity with the poor, marginalized, and dispossessed.

Though devastated by the brutal killing of Grande, Romero harboured neither ill will nor hatred, but continued to preach reconciliation:

> Let there be no animosity in our heart. . . . Let this Eucharist, which is a call to reconciliation with God and our brothers and sisters, leave in all hearts the satisfaction that we are Christians. . . . Let us pray to the Lord for forgiveness and for the due repentance of those who converted a town into a prison and a place of torment.[8]

As a man opposed to violence, Romero believed that those who live by the sword, die by the sword. He pleaded for repentance from the perpetrators so that God's mercy and kindness would fall upon them like the rain and they would all become brothers and sisters.

Romero continued to witness more atrocities committed by the military when he became the archbishop of El Salvador in 1977. Confronting President Carlos Humberto of El Salvador

7. Quoted in Brockman, *Romero*, 10.
8. Quoted in Brockman, *Romero*, 63.

which were confiscated. But his *Meditations on the Stations of the Cross* survived and was made public during his funeral in 2000.[18]

## No Submission to a Godless Regime

Kung was a modest person who never had expected to be made a bishop. In fact, he was upset when he learnt of his episcopal appointment. When he became bishop of the new Diocese of Soochow, Kung adopted a conciliatory approach and was prepared to dialogue with the Communist regime without compromising the fundamental principles of Christianity. In fact, he sought peaceful coexistence of the Catholic Church with the government, hoping to find a middle ground that would allow Catholics to be good citizens as well as faithful Catholics. But the Communists could not acknowledge any distinction that would allow Catholics to be patriotic without adhering to the atheistic ideology of Marxism. Kung wanted peace above all else, but he would not allow a concession that would contradict his faithfulness to the church. The bishop was not lacking in flexibility; it was the lack of clarity on the part of the Communists regarding their goals that was at fault.[19]

Preferring imprisonment and suffering rather than submitting to a godless regime, Kung testified to the reality of God in both Communist China and the capitalist West. The years of privation and pain truly made him a great confessor of the faith. Kung reminds us of Paul's message, "I have fought the good fight, I have finished the race, I have kept the faith" (2 Tim 4:7). In his life, which spanned the twentieth century, Kung bore witness to Christ, his church, and his own fidelity to the successor of St. Peter. But when Kung sang "Tu es Petrus et super hanc petram aedificabo Ecclesiam" at the banquet, Bishop Aloysius Jin chided him. Why?

18. DiGiovanni, *Ignatius*, 85.

19. DiGiovanni, *Ignatius*, 10.

## Naïve, Ineffectual Opposition

While Kung was hailed as a hero by the church, Aloysius Jin maintained that Kung was in fact a "tragic character" who mindlessly obeyed the Vatican by promoting anti-Communist sentiments. Catholics who naively followed Kung's orders and were prepared for martyrdom were not successful in the sense that they were imprisoned for long terms. Kung was jailed for life, but when he was allowed to go to America for medical treatment, he remained in the United States, where he continued to make anti-Communist statements. Although the Vatican made Kung a cardinal, Jin remarked that a good shepherd should remain with his flock and not abandon them. According to Aloysius Jin, Ignatius Kung lost his freedom a second time because he could not speak English and was being controlled by his nephew Kung Minchuan in the United States.[20]

The Communist press propagated Kung's purported apology after his release from prison. Loyal Catholics feared that Kung might be being manipulated by the authorities, especially when he started to make bewildered testimonies. Fearful of the new forces exerted against a wearied old bishop that might ruin his reputation, they wanted to preserve the spirit of his courageous defiance against Communism.[21]

Kung died in Stamford, Connecticut, in 2000 at age ninety-eight. He was buried in the Mission Cemetery in Santa Clara, California. Jin questioned Kung's move to the United States. He believed that Kung's stubbornness was damaging to the church in China. Very much under the control of the French Jesuits, Kung was not popular with the local clergy, Jin claimed. He even accused Kung of being "80 percent French and 20 percent Chinese."[22] Such harsh criticism contradicts the general impression of Kung as a holy, honest, and heroic bishop.

20. Jin, *Memoirs*, 200.

21. Mariani, *Church Militant*, 215.

22. Mariani, *Church Militant*, 216.

## The Balancing Act of Aloysius Jin Luxian

> Aloysius Jin's half-century struggle was aimed at keeping
> Catholicism alive in China, and building a Church for
> "100 million Catholics."[23]

Despite his unfair criticism of his old colleague, Jin was considered brilliant, even by his critics. Through his excellent administration, the battered Diocese of Shanghai was revived with the construction and re-opening of hundreds of parishes. With few religious vocations from Shanghai, Jin recruited seminarians and religious sisters from China's Catholic villages in the interior. With funding from international organizations and missionary societies, Jin was able to build up his diocese.[24]

Nominated by the Chinese Catholic Patriotic Association to lead the officially-sanctioned church, Jin maintained that the only true church was the one regulated by the Patriotic Association.[25] Loyal Catholics found Jin's argument hypocritical and absurd. Jin was consecrated as "patriotic" bishop in 1985, without Vatican approval, a few months after Kung had been released on parole after nearly thirty years in jail. Although Kung was the legitimate bishop, Jin was effectively in charge.

Born on June 20, 1916 in Shanghai, Jin joined the Society of Jesus in 1938 and was ordained a priest in 1945. After two years of pastoral work, he went to Rome and obtained a doctorate from the Gregorian University in 1950. He returned to China at the time when the nation was taken over by the Red Army led by Mao Zedong.

Arrested in the September 8 Incident in 1955, during a major crackdown that included Bishop Ignatius Kung and hundreds of other priests and laity, Jin was sentenced to prison for re-education for twenty-seven years. During these years, he worked as a translator for the government, which included the Public Security Bureau.

23. Minter, "Keeping Faith," 75.

24. Mariani, *Church Militant*, 217–18.

25. Mariani, *Church Militant*, 214.

As early as 1951, after his studies in Rome and return to Shanghai, Jin had offered his frank opinion regarding the political situation in China: he told both Bishop Kung and Bishop Simon Zhu Kai-min that foreign missionaries should leave China because Communism would remain. Thus, the Chinese church should take responsibility for itself, and Catholic bishops should find a way to work with the regime.[26]

When given multiple tasks in the Jesuit community, the diocese and major seminary in Shanghai, Jin "prayed, not hindering tears from falling, without [having] the slightest mettle of a hero." Heroism was not his calling, he admitted, because he had to deal with heavy responsibilities. In his new roles, Jin attempted to address some of the conflicts between the Jesuits and the local diocesan priests. Prepared to hand over more properties to the diocese, he moved the Jesuits out of the parish of St. Joseph's in Yangjingbang.[27] He wanted to strengthen the local church by reducing the control of the Jesuits, an international order, of which he was a member.

After his release from jail in 1982, Jin, unlike Kung, decided to cooperate with the Communist leaders to re-establish the church in Shanghai. He became a powerful bishop, sanctioned by the government. Margaret Chu, the niece of Bishop Kung, was shocked to learn that Jin, who was her spiritual director, had cooperated with the Communists. After Jin was arrested, he recorded a tape to persuade Catholics to support the government. Under pressure, Jin accused Bishop Kung and his followers in his confession.[28] Not surprisingly, his critics called him a traitor, and some Jesuits even denounced him. Bishop Jin was ordained auxiliary bishop without Vatican approval in 1985 and became diocesan bishop of Shanghai in 1988, a position he held until his death in 2013. The Vatican eventually recognized him as apostolic administrator to Bishop Joseph Fan Zhongliang, the bishop of Shanghai, in 2005.[29]

26. Mariani, *Church Militant*, 58.

27. Mariani, *Church Militant*, 136.

28. Mariani, *Church Militant*, 189.

29. UCA News, "Bishop Jin of Shanghai Dead at 96." Several priests from

## Deng Xiaoping's Reforms

While Jin was impressed with the courage and piety of underground Catholic bishops, priests, and laity, he was convinced
that the underground movement would never be able to provide
proper and stable spiritual care for the thousands of Catholics
who attended Mass weekly and openly in Shanghai. After nearly
three decades of incarceration, Jin was determined to establish a
distinctively Chinese church that would replace the missionary
church of his youth, reconciling Catholicism with Chinese cultural
identity. According to a report, Jin was fully released as the result
of the reform programs of then paramount leader Deng Xiaoping.
In fact, Deng opened churches and seminaries and controlled the
activities of the faithful.

Despite criticism from various quarters, Jin always regarded
himself as a faithful member of the Catholic Church and the
Society of Jesus. He once said, "I am both a serpent and a dove.
The government thinks I'm too close to the Vatican, and the Vatican thinks I am too close to the government. I'm a slippery fish
squashed between government control and Vatican demands."[30]

Jin regarded the Catholic Patriotic Association as an important helper and maintained a collaborative relationship with
the government. As a result of his conciliatory approach towards
the authorities, Jin was able to accomplish many things for the
church in China. He re-opened more than one hundred parishes
in Shanghai, established a seminary staffed with competent profes-
sors and equipped with a good library, opened a diocesan publish-
ing house and a retreat center, and sent many priests for further
studies abroad.

Jin was advised by Liu Jun, deputy head of the Political Security Department, to stay away from the underground Catholic
Church. Beijing had begun a new policy of religious freedom and

---

outside China were present at Jin's consecration on January 27, 1985, including Cardinal John Tong of Hong Kong. Hence, there was a possibility that Jin
would be reconciled with Rome eventually. Minter, "Keeping Faith," 82.

30. Jin, *Memoirs*, xvi.

wanted the Chinese people to lead their own churches and not be controlled by foreigners. The days of foreign missionaries were long over. There was thus a need to open seminaries to train the next generation of priests for the church. Liu insisted that Jin had the responsibility to re-establish the church; otherwise, Catholicism would simply fade from China. In other words, Jin would be responsible for the future of the Catholic Church in China.[31]

Jin was thus grateful to the Chinese authorities, especially the Political Security Department and the Shanghai Religious Affairs Bureau, for encouraging him to revive the Catholic Church in Shanghai. The deputy head of the bureau, Chen Yiming, was the one who helped Jin to open churches, reclaim church property, and re-establish the Diocese of Shanghai on a firm foundation.[32]

Considered the most influential and controversial figure in Chinese Catholicism of the last fifty years, Jin persuaded the authorities to allow a prayer for the pope to be recited during Mass in the "open" churches.[33] Rome did not condemn him, probably because he had accomplished a lot in Shanghai and they hoped to enter into dialogue with him. As of 2007, his diocese included 141 registered parishes, 74 priests (most of whom are under 40 years of age), 86 nuns, 83 seminarians and 150,000 faithful. Although he belonged to the official church, Jin was said to have quietly accepted the authority of the Pope in his heart.

Jin thought that the sufferings of the underground church were unnecessary because the sacraments were available in the open or official churches. Accommodation was better than resistance because there was no way that Catholics can confront the Communist authorities and win. "I don't wait for [the Communist] collapse," he said. "I get things done now." Communist secret police, like God, are everywhere, so it is stupid to hide.[34]

31. Jin, *Memoirs*, 284.

32. Jin, *Memoirs*, 285.

33. Minter, "Keeping Faith," 76. Jin was credited for gaining permission from the government to name the pope in the Canon of the Mass and to use liturgical books in Chinese. Wang, "Msgr. Aloysius Jin Luxian."

34. Minter, "Keeping Faith," 76.

## Jin and the Jesuit Detractors

In spite of his practical policy and success as a church builder, Jin had many detractors, especially among the Jesuits, both in Shanghai and abroad. His fiercest critic was his old friend Laszlo Ladany, a Hungarian-born Jesuit who was based in Hong Kong for many years. A China watcher, Ladany believed that foreigners, ignorant of the Communist United Front strategy, were misled by Jin. They wrongly thought that supporting the Patriotic Association might improve the situation of the Catholics.[35]

Many people questioned Jin's sincerity, his ability to keep confidentiality, and his lack of caution, which exposed him to blackmail. Ironically, even though Jin was despised and even hated by the underground church, it was he who sought to protect them, given his influence and contact with the authorities. It is therefore not difficult to understand the rationality behind Jin's willingness to comply with government policies.

Having observed at close range how the French Jesuits and other foreign missionaries, with their ties to colonial powers, had managed the church in China, Jin felt that it was appropriate and expedient to seek protection and even privileges from the state. He believed he could achieve more for the church, giving it stability, by establishing a good relationship with the authorities.[36] Not to be dictated to by foreigners on matters of life and death, Jin wanted a Chinese church that was responsible for its own future.

## Question of Legitimacy

Besides being a controversial character, Jin was also a charming cleric who spoke English, French, and Italian fluently. Over the years, many religious dignitaries, such as Hans Küng, Desmond Tutu, Billy Graham, and Mother Teresa, visited him. But Jin's relationship with the Vatican was initially fraught with difficulties, especially over the question of his legitimacy as bishop of Shanghai.

35. Mariani, *Church Militant*, 218.
36. Mariani, *Church Militant*, 218–19.

It appeared later that Jin was one of the patriotic bishops that had been reconciled with Rome. This was confirmed in 2005 when he was invited by Pope Benedict XVI, together with three others from the mainland, to attend a synod of bishops. It was likely that some welcomed the move by the Vatican to recognize Jin as the official bishop of Shanghai, while others felt betrayed. At any rate, Jin was not given permission by the Chinese government to travel to Rome.[37]

Both Ignatius Kung and Aloysius Jin were arrested on September 8, 1955, together with other priests, nuns, and lay people. Jin was convicted of counter-revolutionary activities and sentenced to twenty-seven years in prison, and Kung was convicted of high treason and sentenced to life in prison. Released from prison, both took different positions regarding the official church and the underground movement; their decisions symbolized the disunity and discord that exist in the Catholic Church in China. This situation still causes confusion, and it is a dilemma for Chinese Catholics struggling to reconcile the underground church with the official one which is associated with an atheistic regime and cut off from the Vatican.

## Be Good Christians and Good Citizens

What should the Catholic Church do? To challenge the Communist Party is foolhardy. The challenge is for the church to redefine its relations with the party, not necessarily agreeing always with its political values, by finding ways and means to cooperate, to accommodate each other, and to build a more humane and equitable society. The church has to work with the government to find ways to continue its pastoral mission.

There are divisions, tensions, and conflicts between the so-called patriotic, official church and the underground Catholic communities, with long-lasting bitter memories that cannot be ignored. Both have suffered grievously, but to move forward, one

37. Mariani, *Church Militant*, 220.

cannot remain bound to the past forever. By the grace of God, through forgiving and the purification of memories, sufferings can bear fruit for reconciliation. The two communities must not allow hatred and injuries from the past to block them from proclaiming the gospel.

One of the Vatican's significant advances was signing a provisional agreement with the People's Republic of China on September 22, 2018, whereby Pope Francis lifted the excommunications of seven bishops. As this agreement concerns the bishop's nomination, it is of great importance for the life of the church and creates further opportunities for future cooperation. The Vatican's Secretary of State, Cardinal Pietro Parolin, asserted that the agreement is particularly significant for the Catholic Church in China regarding dialogue between the Holy See and the Chinese authorities.

Pope Francis is aware Catholics are a "small flock" living during precarious times in China. Some have suffered because of their fidelity to the pontiff and felt that the Holy See had abandoned them. Others are hoping for a better future where the church can flourish. The pontiff expresses his admiration for the Catholics in China and their gift of fidelity and trust in God in adverse and difficult situations. Their sufferings and pain are part of the "spiritual treasury" of the Chinese church and all God's children.[38]

The underground church emerged as a reaction against government-appointed bishops, for appointing bishops is beyond the competence of the state. It is a clandestine Catholic community, which is not normal in church life. Francis knows that many Catholics wish to live their faith in full communion with the pope as a source of unity for the entire church. He has received "numerous concrete signs and testimonies" from them, including from illicit bishops, of their desire for communion in the church.[39]

In an interview, Cardinal Parolin summarized the challenges facing the church in China: "Certainly, there are many wounds still open. To heal them, we need the balm of mercy. And suppose someone is asked to make a sacrifice, small or great. In that case,

38. Francis, "Message of Pope Francis to the Catholics of China," 68.
39. Francis, "Message of Pope Francis to the Catholics of China," 70.

it needs to be clear to all that this is not the price of a political exchange but is part of the Gospel perspective of the greater good, the good of the Church of Christ." We must no longer speak of "legitimate" or "illegitimate," "clandestine" or "official" bishops in China. We need to speak the rhetoric of collaboration and communion.[40]

It is of great significance that when Pope Francis concluded his visit to Mongolia with a Mass on Sunday, September 3, 2023 in Ulaanbaatar, he took a moment to invite Cardinal Tong and Cardinal Stephen Chow, SJ, to the altar holding their hands, he said:

> These are two brother bishops, the emeritus of Hong Kong and the current bishop of Hong Kong. I would like to take advantage of their presence to send a warm greeting to the noble people of China. To all the people I wish the best. Strive ahead, always advancing. And I ask Chinese Catholics to be good Christians and good citizens. Thank you.[41]

Chinese Catholics are urged to be "good citizens" besides being good Christians. Keen to forge a good relationship with the Chinese government through dialogue and constructive engagement, the Vatican wants to ensure that the Catholic faithful can worship in peace and practice their faith freely. Such was the approach of Bishop Aloysius Jin Luxian of Shanghai when he decided to collaborate with the Chinese government so that he could accomplish something for the church rather than languish in jail. While we admire and respect Kung's courage and fidelity, we have to accept that China is now more informed and confident to engage with Western ideas and faith.

Let the past inform our future.

---

40. Spadaro, "Agreement Between China and the Holy See."
41. Watkins, "Pope Francis Urges Chinese Catholics to Be 'Good Citizens.'"

# Chapter 2

# Pedro Arrupe, SJ
## Priest and Prophet

I didn't understand a thing. In fact, what he said seemed to me difficult and obscure. But after a year of carefully observing the father, I said to myself: If Christianity can produce a human being of such great quality, it will also be good for me. The important thing was not what he was saying but what he was living.[1]

THIS WAS THE RESPONSE from an elderly Japanese man when asked why he chose to be baptized by Arrupe. He had completed adult catechism lessons taught by Arrupe for a year and was impressed more by his teacher's character than his class.

Pedro Arrupe's words of "prophet vision and penetrating intuition" inspired many,[2] and the above is one of the numerous examples about Arrupe embodying the gospel he preached. He entirely devoted his life to God and tirelessly served the welfare of people. Instead of relying on mere words, Arrupe left a lasting impact through his actions. He lived with joy and simplicity,

1. Lamet, *Pedro Arrupe*, 2.
2. Lamet, *Pedro Arrupe*, 2.

deeply understanding that evangelization is more about actions than words. The following captures his personality perfectly:

> The plain fact is that the General [Pedro Arrupe] is a captivating human being. Few people can leave his presence without feeling more spring in their step. He is a charismatic figure who has no need of the conventional props and trappings of authority. He assumes no airs and graces, and is devoid of affectation. He is direct, sincere, unassuming, without a hint of patronage or playacting. As a public figure he has learnt, sometimes from mistakes which he looks back on with wry amusement, the need for diplomacy, but he has no natural taste for politics.[3]

Elected as the Superior General in 1965, Arrupe guided the Society of Jesus through the changes of Vatican II, emphasizing working with the poor in the service of faith and the promotion of justice. Recognized for his influence in the church and the world, Arrupe drew attention to the issues of war, peace, poverty, and other social problems. A man of prayer, his indefatigable optimism was rooted in faith and the ability to find all God in all things.

The secret of Arrupe's confidence was his profound faith, which kept him hopeful: "They say I am optimistic, and I think I am. It seems to me a grace of God at this time to have an optimistic temperament. The reason for this optimism is that I have great confidence in God; we are in his hands." His sense of security was accompanied by his humility and simplicity: "I am a poor human who tries to spoil God's work as little as possible."[4] Arrupe held the belief that it is during times of heightened insecurity that the presence of the Lord is particularly near to us.

Returning from a trip to Asia in 1981, he suffered a massive stroke as a result of cerebral thrombosis. In his sickness, he experienced a greater dependence on God until he passed away on February 5, 1991. The beatification of Pedro Arrupe, SJ, was launched in Rome on February 5, 2019.

3. Campbell-Johnston, "Pedro Arrupe Remembered," 78.

4. Lamet, *Pedro Arrupe*, 479.

This chapter examines the significant stages of Pedro Arrupe's life and career when he experienced profound suffering that drew him closer to God and people. His ideas and proposals are still pertinent, particularly in addressing the challenges and difficulties our contemporary world faces. Arrupe emphasized that we cannot solve today's problems with yesterday's solutions. This man was ahead of his time!

## Early Life

Born in Bilbao, Spain, on November 14, 1907, Pedro Arrupe grew up in a caring middle-class family, the youngest child with four sisters. His mother died when he was ten years old, and his father died when he was eighteen. After his secondary schooling, he entered the medical school at the University of Madrid. Arrupe studied medicine for four years with excellent results. During this period, his religious upbringing and character led him to ask questions regarding physical and spiritual sickness.

In 1926, after his father's death, Pedro travelled to Lourdes with his sisters. Since he studied medicine, he was able to offer his services to the Medical Verification Bureau. Arrupe witnessed three miracles at Lourdes. The first was a nun with Pott's disease, a type of tuberculosis that affects the bones. When the paralyzed sister encountered the Blessed Sacrament, Jesus Christ, she was healed: "Crying out, the nun sat up on her stretcher, reached out her arms toward the Eucharist, and fell forward on her knees. 'I am cured!' was all she could say. And the whole crowd shouted in response: 'Miracle!'"[5]

The second miracle involved a seventy-five-year-old woman from Brussels who had stomach cancer and was beyond medical care. She bathed in the water at Lourdes. Afterwards, she could eat, and within three days, the X-rays showed no sign of cancer. She became perfectly healthy.

5. Grogan, *Pedro Arrupe*, 39–40.

The third miracle Arrupe witnessed was a young man with polio. The bishop blessed him with the sign of the cross using the Blessed Sacrament. The young man stood up from the stretcher, and the crowd rejoiced, shouting, "Miracle! Miracle!" Arrupe, a medical student, examined him:

> I felt God so close to me in his miracles that he dragged me violently behind him. And I saw him so close to those who suffer, those who weep, and those whose lives are shattered. An ardent desire burned within me to imitate him in such ready closeness to the world's human debris, to those despised by a society that doesn't suspect that there are souls pulsating beneath such great sorrow.[6]

This profound experience of God at Lourdes led Pedro to leave medical school and join the Society of Jesus in 1927. The Spanish Republic expelled the Jesuits from the country in 1932, and thus Arrupe went into exile in Marneffe, Belgium, with the rest of the Jesuits. Ordained to the priesthood on July 30, 1937, Pedro spent time studying psychiatry in Washington, DC. He finished his fourth year of theology at St. Marys, Kansas, and his tertianship in Cleveland, Ohio.

## Japan 1938–65

After persistent requests, Arrupe went to Japan in 1938 as a missionary. Travelling from the United States to Japan on the eve of the Second World War, he studied Japanese in preparation to work among the people there. Arrupe made a great effort to learn the native tongue, adapting himself to the local culture in a political climate that was difficult for a Westerner. He believed that without understanding the culture and language, there was no way he could preach a Christianity that would take root in Japan.

Arrupe also dedicated himself to studying and practicing Zen meditation, recognizing the significance of comprehending, and adapting, the religious norms of the country of his ministry. Zen,

6. Lamet, *Pedro Arrupe*, 58.

which originated in India during the sixth century and thrived in Japan from the twelfth century onward, offers a means to gain profound insight into one's inner self. Arrupe's commitment to inculturation reflects his humility, respect, and belief in the presence of the Holy Spirit within the culture he was evangelizing. To gain a deeper understanding of Japanese culture, he also studied the underlying philosophy behind practices like the tea ceremony, archery, and flower arrangement.

As the Superior General, Arrupe encouraged his fellow Jesuits to embrace "inculturation." This term refers to embodying Christian life and message within a specific cultural context. It goes beyond mere expression through cultural elements and becomes a driving force that transforms and revitalizes the culture. Arrupe described it as a process that involves assimilating and adopting cultural elements while allowing the Christian message to influence, inspire, and renew the local culture.[7]

Another important Japanese trait that Arrupe learned was that they judge an individual's "interior spirit" by observing his external actions.[8] Arrupe narrates an experience of attempting to catechize adults. An elderly Japanese watched him intensely for six months without saying anything for or against his teaching. Puzzled, Arrupe asked, "What do you think of my explanations?" The man replied, "I cannot give an opinion because I heard nothing. I am completely deaf. However, for me it is sufficient just to look into your eyes. You do not lie. What you believe, I believe also." The authenticity of Arrupe's message and the transparency of his character was enough for the man. Thus, Arrupe was convinced that evangelization "involves *being* more than speaking."[9]

This stage of his life in Japan included moments of suffering and consolation, both within his experience of the Eucharist. Writing about the joy of celebrating mass on the summit of Mount Fuji at dawn, Arrupe also revealed the spiritual suffering he endured when deprived of the Eucharist for thirty-three days in a Japanese

7. De Souza, "Process of Inculturation," 631–32.

8. Grogan, *Pedro Arrupe*, 57.

9. Lamet, *Pedro Arrupe*, 479.

jail. After the bombing of Pearl Harbour on December 7, 1941, Arrupe was arrested by Japanese security forces and kept in solitary confinement. When the security forces came to release him, he thought they were going to execute him. The experience in prison led him to a deeper trust in God.

## Solitary Confinement

The increasing conflict between Japan and the United States resulted in war, and Arrupe's visit to the States had made him a person to suspect. Following the Japanese bombing of Pearl Harbour in December 1941, Arrupe was arrested on espionage charges by the Japanese military police, the Kempetai. Thrown into a small cell with rats and walls stained with blood, Arrupe later remembered that "it was very cold. One could not sleep; I was shivering and my teeth were chattering. There is absolute silence. The hours pass with the increased slowness of waiting."[10] He endured thirty-three days in solitary confinement, where he was forbidden to celebrate Mass and deprived of human companionship. Experiencing deep pain due to the lack of the Eucharist, Arrupe also acknowledged the faithful and consoling presence of the Lord. He wrote:

> What loneliness there was! I then appreciated what the Eucharist means to a priest, to a Jesuit, for whom the Mass and the tabernacle are the very centre of his life. . . . I believe that it was the month in which I learned the most in all my life.[11]

During this period of anguish and loneliness, Arrupe understood more profoundly what Jesus said, "Remember the words that I said to you, 'Servants are not greater than their master. If they persecuted me, they will persecute you too; if they kept my word, they will keep yours also" (John 15:20). Interrogated for thirty-six hours in a row, Arrupe was amazed by his appropriate responses which testified to the truth of the gospel: "So make up

10. Menkhaus, "Lessons from the Spirit," 11.
11. Burke, *Pedro Arrupe*, 56.

your minds not to prepare your defense in advance; for I will give you words and a wisdom that none of your opponents will be able to withstand or contradict" (Luke 21:14–15).

When Arrupe's suffering became more intense, he experienced a moment of consolation. Recalling the many Masses he said on Christmas night, he felt so sad that he was not able to do so in prison. Suddenly, he heard voices outside his prison wall, people singing a Christmas carol, one of the songs he had taught to his followers:

> Suddenly, above the murmur that was reaching me, there arose a soft, sweet, consoling Christmas carol, one of the songs which I had myself taught to my Christians. I was unable to contain myself. I burst into tears. They were my Christians who, heedless of the danger of being themselves imprisoned, had come to console me, to console their *Shimpu Sama* (their priest), who was away that Christmas night which hitherto we had always celebrated with such great joy. What a contrast between that thoughtfulness and the injustice of senseless imprisonment.[12]

The singing lasted but a few minutes and then gone, but Arrupe was deeply touched. It was the best spiritual communion in his life.

When released from prison, Arrupe told his guards and the governor, to their astonishment, that they had done him a service: "You have taught me to suffer. I came to Japan to suffer for the Japanese people. Jesus Christ suffered more than any other man. The believer is not afraid to suffer with or like Christ. You have helped me to understand this."[13] Arrupe later discovered that he was imprisoned because of rumors against him, but he refused to reveal any information to the US crime investigators. He wanted to forgive and move on towards healing.

---

12. Burke, *Pedro Arrupe*, 57.
13. Menkhaus, "Lessons from the Spirit," 10.

## The Hiroshima Physician

Soon after his release from jail in 1942, Arrupe was sent to Nagatsuka, just outside of Hiroshima, to assume his duties as novice master. On that fateful day of August 6, 1945, he witnessed the enormous explosion of the atomic bomb, which shattered the doors and windows of his residence. The atomic bomb dropped on the city of Hiroshima was a devastating blast that changed the course of history. He wrote:

> I shall never forget my first sight of what was the result of the atomic bomb: a group of young women, eighteen or twenty years old, clinging to one another as they dragged themselves along the road. One had a blister that almost covered her chest; she had burns across half of her face and a cut in her scalp caused probably by a falling tile, while great quantities of blood coursed freely down her face. On and on they came, a steady procession numbering some 150,000. This gives some idea of the scene of horror that was Hiroshima.[14]

With his medical skills, Arrupe was able to treat the wounds and injuries of about 150 people suffering from the toxic effects of radiation in their small homes. He said, "The suffering was frightful, the pain excruciating, and it made bodies writhe like snakes, yet there was not a word of complaint."[15] Later, Arrupe led a rescue team into Hiroshima and brought home those who were burned, blinded, deafened, and skinned. They were warned by the authorities not to enter the ravaged city, but the Jesuit helpers went anyway, took care of the casualties, and helped to cremate fifty thousand corpses.[16] The encounter with the victims of Hiroshima taught Pedro Arrupe many lessons about the human person and the destructive power of violence. The experience of Hiroshima moved him to use all his energy to alleviate human suffering.

---

14. Burke, *Pedro Arrupe*, 41.
15. Menkhaus, "Lessons from the Spirit," 13.
16. Grogan, *Pedro Arrupe*, 64.

The dropping of the atomic bomb on the innocent in Hiroshima shocked Arrupe profoundly as it revealed to him the deep gulf between good and evil, between God's handiwork and the human destruction of it. Humanity, he wrote, "is trapped in a net of steel, out of which it is difficult to break."[17] Years later, Arrupe asserted that the "apocalypse of Hiroshima" transformed his life, deepened his dependence on God and revealed "what is deadly and truly terrible about force and violence."[18] Opposed to any form of violence, Arrupe would later criticize those who took up arms against unjust regimes.

Recalling that fateful morning of August 6, 1945, Arrupe wrote, "History is truly the teacher of life, but only on condition that we know how to interpret her."[19] Thus, humanity must continue to read the signs of the times. As a survivor of the atomic bomb, Arrupe had written a reflection that remains relevant and prophetic for the twenty-first century: "It is not just a memory, but a perpetually vital event outside history, which does not go away with the ticking of the clock."[20] Remembering the horrors and the suffering of the innocents, Arrupe specified two issues that are still threatening our society today: unjust social structures and weapons of mass destruction.

## Unjust Social Structures

Arrupe's reflection focused on the unjust social structures that trap people in marginalized and hungry conditions. He emphasized that over half of humanity suffers from undernourishment, and the situation in underdeveloped countries worsens every day. Arrupe concluded that a significant portion of society bears responsibility for this "sinful" state of affairs. While individuals may hold moral perspectives, the priorities of national development or

17. Burke, *Pedro Arrupe*, 191.
18. Burke, *Pedro Arrupe*, 20.
19. Menkhaus, "Lessons from the Spirit," 9.
20. Menkhaus, "Lessons from the Spirit," 15.

economic systems often overshadow their responsibility towards the impoverished and marginalized in society.[21]

Pope Francis, a Jesuit close to Arrupe, highlights the new economy of exclusion. This economy disregards people, treating them as mere leftovers in society: "How can it be that it is not a news item when an elderly homeless person dies of exposure, but it is news when the stock market loses two points? This is a case of exclusion. Can we continue to stand by when food is thrown away while people are starving? This is a case of inequality."[22]

Like Arrupe, the pontiff challenges people to be more aware of the waste of food and resources in our society. Pope Francis characterized the modern mentality as "a globalization of indifference . . . incapable of feeling compassion at the outcry of the poor, weeping for other people's pain . . . as though all this were someone else's responsibility."[23] Pope Francis's condemnation of our modern indifference towards the sufferings of others echoes Arrupe's strong criticism of the way the victims of the atomic bomb were treated as just an unfortunate incident.

In his encyclical *Laudato Si'* (On Care for Our Common Home), Pope Francis also criticizes the global indifference towards the destruction of the environment. He urges people to be more aware of how their actions and behaviors affect the common good, the earth, and our shared home. The pope warns, "The [global] warming caused by huge consumption on the part of some rich countries has repercussions on the poorest areas of the world."[24] Throughout the document, Francis's concern for the poor and the effect of climate change on poor nations is evident. While Arrupe's understanding of climate change was limited during his time, Pope Francis's concerns align closely with Arrupe's reflections on wealthy nations' responsibility towards the poor and marginalized.

This concern for the poor goes back to Arrupe's student days in Madrid in the 1920s when he was a member of the Society of St.

21. Menkhaus, "Lessons from the Spirit," 15.
22. Francis, *Evangelii Gaudium*, 53.
23. Francis, *Evangelii Gaudium*, 54.
24. Francis, *Laudato Si'*, 51.

Vincent de Paul. During his visits to a slum, he witnessed the difficult circumstances faced by widows, malnourished children, and the sick who were begging for help. These encounters unveiled for him the deep-rooted inequality within our economic and social systems. His first exposure to societal injustice ignited his passion to advocate for the poor. As he continued to witness more instances of poverty and injustice, his concern for the marginalized and outcasts in society grew even stronger. This concern for the poor became a central aspect of Arrupe's priestly ministry; he dedicated himself to serving others, particularly those at the bottom of the social ladder. Arrupe firmly believed that God's presence is most evident in the lives of the poor.[25]

## Weapons of Mass Destruction

Twenty-five years after Hiroshima, Arrupe warned against the continued possession of weapons of mass destruction by governments. He emphasized that eliminating them is the only way to ensure their non-usage. Today, nuclear weapons are within reach of more nations than ever before, with the potential for devastating consequences. The negotiations between Iran and Western powers in 2015 highlighted the urgent need to prevent nuclear proliferation. This issue remains a constant threat in the ongoing debate regarding the threat of nuclear war.[26]

While many countries still possess nuclear weapons, a new technology presents a more immediate danger. The skies over Afghanistan, Pakistan, Iraq, Syria, and other Middle Eastern countries are filled with thousands of drones sent by the US and other Western countries. Their purpose is to combat militant groups like al-Qaeda and ISIS. However, drones have caused civilian deaths in these countries, even without an official declaration of war. The exact number of civilian casualties varies, but drones have unquestionably caused hundreds of deaths in Somalia, Yemen, and

---

25. Lamet, *Pedro Arrupe*, 39–43.
26. Menkhaus, "Lessons from the Spirit," 17–18.

Pakistan. Many civilians in the West, however, support the use of drones in war because it reduces the risk of losing their soldiers in battle.[27]

Atomic bombs have not been used in war since 1945 due to their immense power and the fear of mutual destruction. The Hiroshima bomb alone claimed the lives of over a hundred thousand people in a single blast, and modern nuclear warheads are even more devastating. Checks and balances have increased since Arrupe's time. Nonetheless, drones have now emerged as a new form of danger and a silent killer. Unlike nuclear weapons, which have inherent limitations due to their complexity, the use of drones tends to escalate as more countries acquire the technology to kill from a distance without jeopardizing their safety.[28]

In his address at the opening of the Third Inter-American Congress of Religious in Montreal on November 21, 1977, Pedro Arrupe spoke about the current state of the world. Arrupe recognized our progress in various areas, such as the material, scientific, technological, theological, humanistic, and ethical. However, he acknowledged that poverty and war still threaten our world. Arrupe believed that the only way to end war was by addressing hunger and malnutrition and promoting human dignity. Disrespect for human beings stems from injustice and oppression. Arrupe also expressed concern about the growing population and the uncontrollable proliferation of nuclear powers. He stated that if present trends continue, the situation in the year 2000 would be much worse, with the rich becoming richer and the poor becoming poorer. The gap between the rich and the poor, both in terms of numbers and living standards, will have become enormous.[29]

---

27. Menkhaus, "Lessons from the Spirit," 18.
28. Menkhaus, "Lessons from the Spirit," 18.
29. Arrupe, "New Lesson," 377.

## *Homo Consumens*

Arrupe expressed concern about the prevalence of consumerism among a significant portion of individuals in affluent nations. He observed that people in these countries, influenced by advertising from a young age, had become conditioned to purchase and consume various goods incessantly. This transformation has caused a shift in our species from being *homo sapiens* to *homo consumens*. Both consumers and advertisers influence the economy, perpetuating and justifying the desire for more and greater material possessions. Arrupe noted that what was once considered superfluous has become convenient, what was convenient has become necessary, and what was necessary has become indispensable. The study of advertising techniques reveals their objective to penetrate our unconscious minds, manipulating our psychology and decision-making processes. Consequently, we have experienced a loss of our freedom to act independently and rationally.[30]

Business corporations are not content with simply conditioning consumers; they aim to establish a consumer society that embraces consumerist values, attitudes, and laws while promoting class superiority. Their concept of freedom revolves around unrestricted consumption of goods and services, equating development with the accumulation of more goods, industrialization, urbanization, and higher per capita income. Their notion of freedom of information centers on expanding the market, maximizing profits, and transforming the global village into a company town. The focus is on the self, viewing others as mere means to serve individual purposes. The driving motive is profit, with efficiency as the prevailing moral norm. They employ any means necessary to achieve their primary goal: profit.[31]

---

30. Arrupe, "New Service," 377.
31. Arrupe, "New Service," 377.

## Homo Serviens

Arrupe emphasized the need to combat consumerism by creating a "society of sufficiency" through a frugal and austere lifestyle. This is crucial for humanity's survival, both materially and socially. Even Marxist leaders recognize the significance of austerity, as they promote values like rigor, efficiency, sobriety, and justice. A politics of austerity aimed at eliminating waste is essential for everyone. Guided by gospel values, Arrupe believed that it is possible to create a just and balanced society by educating individuals to shift from being *homo consumens* (self-centered and materialistic) to *homo serviens* (service-oriented). Driven by possessions, the *homo consumens* is unsatisfied, envious, and greedy. On the other hand, the *homo serviens* seeks to serve others in solidarity, valuing sufficiency over accumulation. Arrupe urges religious sisters, brothers, and priests to embrace lives of service, embodying frugality, and austerity.[32]

Arrupe believed humans could create a just world, but they chose not to. Inequalities and injustices are not caused by the "fatalism of nature," but by human self-centeredness. Blaming multinational corporations and political powers for the existence of structured and institutionalized injustice is easy. Arrupe reminded us that Christians have either built or promoted these systems or are passive consumers. Insensitive governments prioritize their interests over the common good and have failed to address injustices because their citizens are unwilling to make sacrifices and live more modestly to alleviate poverty in the developing world. Arrupe also encouraged us to explore non-violent alternatives to pursue justice and rights.[33]

## Final Notable Achievement

Pedro Arrupe's final notable achievement was the establishment of the Jesuit Refugee Service in 1980. During his travels in Asia,

32. Arrupe, "New Service," 378–79.
33. Arrupe, "New Service," 376.

he witnessed the dire situation of Vietnamese refugees who were fleeing the oppressive Vietnamese Communist regime after the war. This mass exodus marked one of the largest displacements in modern history. Arrupe successfully laid the groundwork for the Jesuit Refugee Service with support from governments and international organizations. The organization's mission was to provide assistance, support, and advocacy for refugees and forcibly displaced individuals.

Unfortunately, in July 1981, Arrupe suffered a massive stroke while returning to Rome from the Philippines. This stroke left him partially paralyzed and severely impaired his speech. Unable to fulfill his duties as Superior General of the Jesuits, Arrupe decided to resign. However, the pope did not formally accept his resignation until two years later. During this time, Pope John Paul II appointed Paolo Dezza, an older Jesuit, to oversee the Society of Jesus during those challenging times. It seemed that Pedro Arrupe and his administration were pushed aside. Nevertheless, Arrupe accepted this with humility and obedience. The infirmarian, Br. Rafael Bandera, remarked, "It was a difficult moment, but Don Pedro demonstrated what he had been and still was."[34] After about thirty minutes, his face and eyes regained their usual demeanor: he smiled with serenity and profound peace.[35]

After a productive sixteen-year tenure in office from 1965 to 1981, Arrupe spent the following decade in silence at the Jesuit infirmary in Rome. This transition must have been difficult for someone known for his eloquence and extensive travels around the world. Despite his later limitations, Arrupe's earlier active years inspired many, while his silence also provided strength to those facing their struggles. Nevertheless, Arrupe faced internal challenges in accepting his condition and the realization that he was entirely dependent on God. It is worth noting that the grace of God can be experienced in both success and victory, as well as in failure and inability.

34. Lamet, *Pedro Arrupe*, 419.
35. Lamet, *Pedro Arrupe*, 419–20.

## An Indomitable Spirit in Suffering and Death

In February 1984, Pope John Paul II authored an apostolic letter titled *The Christian Meaning of Suffering*. The central theme of this letter revolves around the passion of Christ, in which the pope reflects upon love, power, hope, goodness, and grace. According to the pope, suffering can be a catalyst for releasing love. Through the crucifixion and resurrection, new understanding is shed on the darkness of suffering, leading to participation in Christ's redemption of the world. Additionally, the pope emphasizes that suffering can pave the way for grace, bringing about a transformative effect on our souls. It is through the experience of suffering that God's power is revealed, as it liberates us from self-centeredness.[36]

Arrupe could easily identify with the pope's thoughts on suffering. He did not complain. Despite his suffering, he held onto his faith. Bandera, who cared for Arrupe in his illness, observed his patient endurance of suffering. Additionally, Arrupe went through periods of depression and endured the emptiness that comes with illness: "I am alone, terrible, terrible; I am no use at all. I used to speak five languages, and now I cannot express myself in Spanish. Everybody treats me kindly, but in my depths I am alone, alone."[37]

In a homily read by Giuseppe Pittau on May 27, 1982, Arrupe expressed that in this challenging phase of his life, he felt a deep connection with the Lord, whom he has dedicated his life to serving. He entrusts his shortcomings to the boundless mercy of the Lord's heart, knowing he is understood and loved. During the extended periods of inactivity he faced, he was taking the opportunity to reflect on his past and present. In doing so, he actively sought to cooperate with divine grace, following the path of continual purification and conversion that he consistently encouraged the Society of Jesus to embrace.[38]

Despite being physically broken, Arrupe displayed an indomitable spirit. He said, "More than ever, I find myself in the hands

36. Grogan, *Pedro Arrupe*, 177.
37. Lamet, *Pedro Arrupe*, 432.
38. Lamet, *Pedro Arrupe*, 430.

of God. This is what I have wanted all my life, from my youth. But now there is a difference: the initiative is entirely with God. It is indeed a profound spiritual experience to know and feel myself so totally in his hands."[39]

Arrupe's condition worsened significantly after 1985. He was unable to speak, but his life still held meaning. Pope John Paul II visited Arrupe as he neared death, offering silent prayers and his blessing. If Arrupe had been aware of this, it would have been a great source of comfort for him, given his deep reverence for the papacy. When Arrupe passed away, the pope praised the deceased Jesuit for his profound piety, unwavering dedication to the church, and gracious acceptance of God's will in his suffering.[40]

Pedro Arrupe approached death without fear, eagerly anticipating the opportunity to meet the God he loved and served. In his book, *One Jesuit's Spiritual Journey*, Arrupe reflected on the significance of death, viewing it as a meaningful event that would give purpose to his life. He saw death as the gateway to an unknown and desired eternity, a chance to encounter the Lord and experience an eternal closeness with him. Arrupe did not perceive death as a plunge into nothingness but rather as a surrender into the loving embrace of the Lord, who would welcome him with the words, "Well done, good and trustworthy servant; you have been faithful with a few things, I will put you in charge of many things; enter into the joy of your master" (Matt 25:21).[41]

39. Burke, *Pedro Arrupe*, 201.

40. Grogan, *Pedro Arrupe*, 193–94.

41. Based on conversations in 1981 with another Jesuit, Jean-Paul Dietsch, this work was published in 1982 in French and later translated into English. See Arrupe, *One Jesuit's Spiritual Journey*.

## Chapter 3

# The Crucified People
## Voice of Óscar Romero

EL SALVADOR WAS THE name given to the city and future nation by the Spanish conquistador Pedro de Alvarado in honor of Jesus, the Savior of the world. Mirroring the life and death of Jesus, many people in this country, especially the poor and indigenous population, have been cruelly treated and died under the weight of colonial exploitation, social injustice, and despotic rule. These victims who lived in poverty and were massacred in death are the "crucified people." Ignacio Ellacuría, one of the Jesuits murdered by the Salvadoran regime in 1989, taught that:

> This crucified people are the historical continuation of the servant of Yahweh, whom the sin of the world continues to deprive of any human features, which the powers of this world continue stripping of everything, wresting his life from him as long as he lives.[1]

This chapter examines the life and teaching of Archbishop Óscar Romero (1917–80) as the voice of the crucified people. In a nation torn by conflict and violence, Romero preached forgiveness

---

1. Quoted in Sobrino, "Our World," 18. The material in this chapter appeared in Mong, "Crucified People"; Mong, *Forgiven but Not Forgotten*, 89–114.

and reconciliation, convinced that peace can only exist when there is justice and truth. Thus his death inspired the church to redefine its understanding of martyrdom in modern times.

## Be a Patriot. Kill a Priest

In the 1970s, groups of teachers, students, workers, priests, and religious brothers and sisters began to organize themselves and demand a more equitable sharing of wealth and resources in the nation. In the rural areas, peasants organized themselves and demanded fairer wages, land distribution, and better living conditions. The main peasant groups, led by Catholics activists, were the Christian Peasants' Federation (FECCAS) and the Union of Farmworkers (UTC). Fighting for social justice, they established bases for Christian communities and other pastoral and education programs. Quite a few priests and sisters actively encouraged their flock to participate in these popular movements.

Progressive candidates were elected as presidents in 1972 and 1977, but they were unfairly disqualified by the existing regimes amid substantial election fraud. Government-backed right-wing death squads began to assassinate opposition activists and community and church leaders. These death squads consisted of heavily armed soldiers, police, and National Guardsmen in civilian clothes. Some of them were members of ORDEN, a paramilitary group founded by National Guardsmen and the notorious White Warriors' Union. One of their slogans was "Be a Patriot. Kill a Priest," an assignment which they carried out frequently. These death squads sought to repress activists, divide the opposition, and create a "culture of fear" by their random killings.[2]

The Farabundo Marti Front for National Liberation (FMLN), consisting of students, teachers, factory and farm workers, and former government officials, was established in 1980 to fight against the government by armed resistance. It was named after a militant attorney who led Salvadoran peasants during the 1920s

2. Peterson, *Martyrdom and the Politics of Religion*, 63, 33.

and was killed in the *Mantanza* (Slaughter), an uprising that was brutally suppressed by the military. The FMLN wanted to establish a democratic government that was inclusive and willing to accept the cooperation of different political organizations. They demanded that the perpetrators involved in kidnapping and murder be prosecuted and convicted before they would lay down their arms. In addition, the FMLN advocated land reforms and a mixed economy.

Sadly, increased resistance from the FMLN followed by intensified state repression led to a full-fledged civil war. The El Salvador military was determined to eliminate the FMLN's sphere of influence with large-scale bombing, resulting in displacing a quarter of the nation's population. The civil war divided the country geographically into three different kinds of territory: government-controlled zones, mostly in the cities; a conflict zone, where the FLMN and the government army fought for control; and "liberated zones," in the mountains and coastal areas, controlled by the FLMN.[3]

The United States government considered the FMLN a "terrorist organization" because it was financially supported by the Soviet Union and had close connections to the socialist governments in Cuba and Nicaragua. In spite of documented gross human rights abuses by the government of El Salvador, including the killing of US citizens, the Carter, Reagan, and Bush administrations supported it throughout the 1980s in the hope of eliminating the "Communist" FMLN.[4] Between 1980 and 1990, the Salvadoran government received over four billion dollars in US aid, military training, and military advice, which enabled the army to launch a brutal counterinsurgency war on the rural areas controlled by the FLMN. Aerial bombings and mortar attacks in the 1980s killed more civilians than the guerillas.[5] Shortly before his death in 1980,

3. Peterson, *Martyrdom and the Politics of Religion*, 36.

4. The Reagan and Bush administrations called the military regime in El Salvador the "good guys." See "Truth or Consequences in El Salvador," 3.

5. Peterson, *Martyrdom and the Politics of Religion*, 35–36.

Archbishop Óscar Romero wrote to President Carter pleading with him to stop supporting the murderous regime in his country.

Nonetheless, with around thirteen thousand regular fighters in addition to some forty thousand part-time militia members mostly in the rural areas, the FMLN had developed into a formidable force. Widely supported by the civilian population and with good military strategies, the FMLN were able to maintain a stalemate with the government forces. Though relatively small in numbers and with inferior arms, the guerillas were highly motivated compared to the government forces.

On November 11, 1989, the FMLN launched a nation-wide assault and held the capital city, San Salvador, for weeks. Determined to crush the insurgency at all costs, the government ordered aerial bombing of urban areas and arrested scores of activists. Entering the campus of Central American University (UCA), the military killed six Jesuit priests, leading intellectuals in El Salvador who were vocal critics of the government, and their two housekeepers.

The 1989 offensive proved to be a turning point in the history of El Salvador. The killing of the Jesuits and their two helpers at UCA sparked off international outrage and prompted the US government to support peaceful negotiation rather than training the Salvadoran army. Criticizing the US assistance to the military in El Salvador, Fr. Joseph A. O'Hare SJ, president of Fordham University, asked this question in 1989, "Can we hand weapons to butchers and remain unstained by the blood of their innocent victims?"[6] The killing of the Jesuits reveals the Roman Catholic Church's deep involvement in the struggle for justice and peace on behalf of the poor in the nation. It was also evident in the brutal murder of Óscar Romero, which made a deep impact on the people and on the Jesuits who worked at UCA at that time.

6. "Is Justice Still a Long-Way Off for Jesuit Martyrs in El Salvador?" 3.

# Óscar Arnulfo Romero

Born on August 15, 1917, in Ciudad Barrios, El Salvador, Óscar Romero came from a humble family. Since his parents could not afford to send him to school after the age of twelve, he worked as an apprentice carpenter. Determined to become a priest, Romero entered the seminary at the age of fourteen and was ordained in 1942 when he was twenty-five years old. Realizing the power of transistor radio, he attempted to reach out to the peasant farmers by broadcasting his Sunday homilies through radio stations. In 1970, he was made the auxiliary bishop in San Salvador, and in 1974, the bishop of Santiago de Maria.

A traditionalist, Romero supported the hierarchy and conformity to church teachings. He was against political activism that challenged the government. In fact, when news came from Rome that Romero had been chosen to succeed Archbishop Chávez, the government of El Salvador and the oligarchy were very pleased. They believed that Romero, being a conservative, would not threaten their status quo. Most clergy in the archdiocese, however, were disappointed; they thought that Romero was more keen to maintain good relations with the government than to serve the needs of the people. They were mistaken. Soon Romero proved his mettle by championing the rights of the poor and downtrodden. It was not a sudden change, but a gradual transformation as he began to notice the social reality in El Salvador.

After two years as bishop of Santiago de Maria, Romero understood that the social injustice existing in Salvadoran society was the root cause of all its evils. For example, he witnessed children dying because their parents were too poor to seek medical help. Using the resources of his diocese, Romero began to help the poor. Over time, he realized that charity was not enough. To dismantle unjust economic and social structures, there must be a conversion of hearts. Convinced that the Spirit was speaking through the suffering of the people, he defended activist priests fighting for the rights of the poor. When Rutilio Grande, a Jesuit working for the

regarding human rights violations, he became the "voice of the voiceless," one who offered his people faith and hope for a better life.[9] He defended progressive priests, religious sisters, and lay persons who dared to denounce the atrocities of the authorities. Visiting churches in his archdiocese, especially those harassed by the military in the rural areas, such as Chalatenango and Aguilares, Romero also made a passionate plea for the rights of his people to protest. During Sunday homilies in the cathedral, he denounced the brutality of the army and greed of the government as well as the oligarchy, those who controlled most of the country's natural resources.

An outspoken vocal critic of the violent activities of right-wing groups, as well as the leftist guerillas, Romero began to raise global awareness with reports on the murder, torture, and kidnapping that were rampant throughout the country. Addressing soldiers and policemen, Romero cried, "I beg you, I implore you, I order you . . . in the name of God, stop the repression!"[10] Unfortunately, his pleading fell on deaf ears. Yet he never gave up working towards peace and reconciliation in his country. He avoided partisan political positions and advised his priests to do the same. Viewing the country's division and the church's involvement in the unrest as social rather than ideological, Romero held that the conflict was not between the church and the state, but between the state and the people. The church stood with the people because the people are with the church.[11]

In order to restore trust and confidence between the church and the state, Romero was prepared to engage in dialogue with the government. He wanted the authorities in El Salvador to account for the disappearance of persons, to end torture and arbitrary arrests, and to provide due process for priests who were expelled.[12] In setting the conditions for a successful dialogue with the authorities, Romero wanted all sides to be present and all violence to

9. Caritas Australia, "Saint Oscar Romero Biography."

10. Caritas Australia, "Saint Oscar Romero Biography."

11. Peterson, *Martyrdom and the Politics of Religion*, 62.

12. Brockman, *Romero*, 84.

cease, especially government repression of civilians. The subject for dialogue was the call to dismantle unjust structures that promote violence. Terrorists and those who supported violence would lay down their arms if they had a sincere desire for dialogue. Romero emphasized the critical importance of protecting the freedom of expression through various labor organizations—these would be the signs of the presence of democracy in El Salvador.

Romero's outspoken defense of the poor and victims of violence made him a target of violence. In the face of threats to his life, he declared his willingness to sacrifice himself for the "redemption and resurrection" of El Salvador.[13] Ironically, the president of El Salvador offered protection by providing Romero with security guards and an armored car. Romero politely rejected this offer of protection, and wrote to the government in 1979: "I wouldn't accept that protection, because I wanted to run the same risks that the people are running; it would be a pastoral anti-testimony if I were very secure, while my people are so insecure."[14] Instead, Romero took the opportunity to ask the president for protection for the people, especially at military checkpoints and roadblocks.

Like most people, Romero was afraid of violent death, but he never neglected his duty and responsibility in accompanying his flock when they were in danger. Neither did he seek protection for his priests. He said:

> How sad it would be, in a country where such horrible murders are being committed, if there were no priests among the victims! A murdered priest is a testimonial of a church incarnate in the problems of the people.[15]

Persecution produces Christian hope for the church.

Two weeks before his death, Romero had already forgiven his killers:

13. *Encyclopedia Britannica Online*, s.v. "St. Óscar Romero," https://www.britannica.com/biography/Oscar-Arnulfo-Romero.

14. Quoted in Peterson, *Martyrdom and the Politics of Religion*, 62.

15. McDermott, "In the Footsteps of Martyrs," 19.

If they kill me, I will rise again in the people of El Salvador. . . . You can tell them, if they succeed in killing me,
that I pardon them, and I bless those who may carry out
the killing. But I wish that they could realize that they are
wasting their time. A bishop will die, but the church of
God—the people—will never die.[16]

Just before his death, Romero uttered these prophetic words:
"Those who surrender to the service of the poor through love of
Christ will live like the grain of wheat that dies. . . . The harvest
comes because of the grain that dies."[17] On March 24, 1980, while
celebrating Mass in the chapel of Divine Providence Hospital,
Óscar Romero was gunned down by an assassin belonging to a
right-wing death squad.

In spite of prevailing violence, tens of thousands of mourn-
ers attended Romero's funeral, transforming the service into one
of the biggest demonstrations the country had ever witnessed.
Romero lives on in the lives and memories of his people, especially
among the poor with whom he identified himself. Even before his
beatification, the people considered Romero a martyr.

## Violence Against the Church

The repression of peasant movements and popular organizations
leading to the killing of thousands of the indigenous people has
taken place in Latin America since colonial days. But persecution
of the church was a recent phenomenon, given the fact that Roman Catholicism was the dominant religion in the continent. This
attack on the church coincided with the church's teaching on the
preferential option for the poor in the 1960s and the establishment
of base Christian communities.[18] As a result, thousands of Catholic activists, clerics, religious, and lay persons were imprisoned,
tortured, and murdered by the military for their involvement in
fighting for justice and equitable distribution of land. Between

16. Closkey and Hogan, "Introduction," 5.
17. Caritas Australia, "Saint Oscar Romero Biography."
18. Peterson, *Martyrdom and the Politics of Religion*, 63.

1971 and 1990, more than forty religious sisters and priests, as well as one archbishop were killed. Most of these murders took place in El Salvador.

Archbishop Óscar Romero and the other activists were assassinated not for their faith but for denouncing the government and the elites in El Salvador, who were responsible for running a country that systematically exploited the poor for their own advantage. Romero said, "Our church is persecuted precisely for its preferential option for the poor and for trying to incarnate itself in the interest of the poor."[19] The victims were mostly the poor and those who defended them. The attack on the clergy led to widespread persecution of the Christian community.

The conservative establishment in El Salvador, including many bishops, insisted that this attack was committed in retaliation for Romero's political involvement. They blamed left-wing Catholics for getting involved in politics and thus incurring the wrath of the government and the military. Romero, they maintained, should not have gotten involved in politics but instead confined himself to the spiritual care of his flock. In fact, even sympathetic citizens in El Salvador interpreted the attack on the church as politically motivated. The oligarchy colluding with the government and the military sought to crush all opposition, whether secular or religious. The growth of base Christian communities, led by the clergy and lay leaders, became a threat to the established order. Hence, some were brutally killed by death squads not because they were Catholics but because they threatened the wealth and privileges of the elites. As such, can these Catholics, priests and laity, who were murdered because they stood by the side of the oppressed and downtrodden be regarded as martyrs in the church or of the church?

---

19. Quoted in Peterson, *Martyrdom and the Politics of Religion*, 62.

## Martyrdom

In twentieth-century Latin America, many Christians who fought for justice died at the hands of their fellow Christians because of differences in political ideology. Can these be regarded as martyrs in the Catholic tradition? Óscar Romero and Rutilio Grande were killed by death squads in El Salvador—were they Christian martyrs or victims of political assassinations? In a broad sense, they were martyrs who died struggling for justice on behalf of the poor against a ruthless military regime. Even though they may also have been baptized Catholics, the leaders who ordered the killings and those who carried out their orders were anything but Christian. Victims of repression in Latin America have inspired the church to expand and re-define the meaning of Christian martyrdom.

In light of the situation in Latin America, Karl Rahner argued that someone who dies fighting for a cause related to his or her Christian conviction can be regarded as a martyr, provided the death is not directly sought. Of course, not everybody who dies fighting on the Christian or Catholic side in a religious war should be considered one. In Rahner's opinion, someone such as Romero who died while fighting for social justice owing to his profound Christian convictions should be considered a martyr. Rahner thus regarded Christians who died struggling for justice and other Christian virtues as martyrs. His notion differs from the traditional understanding that a martyr is someone who died for his or her faith, such as the Christians in the early church who were brought to court and sentenced to death. In favor of a legitimate political theology, Rahner called upon the church to be aware of its responsibility to promote justice and peace in society.[20]

John Paul II had in fact broadened the term "martyr" in his 1995 encyclical, *Ut Unum Sint* (On Commitment to Ecumenism):

> In a theocentric vision, we Christians already have a common Martyrology. This also includes the martyrs of our own century, more numerous than one might think, and it shows how, at a profound level, God preserves

20. Rahner, "Dimensions of Martrydom," 10.

communion among the baptized in the supreme demand
of faith, manifested in the sacrifice of life itself.[21]

These martyrs include religious (priests, brothers, and sisters) who were killed during the Spanish Civil War (1936–39) and in the Nazi concentration camps. In Latin America, there were many who died as Christians protesting against the atrocities of military dictatorship. Faithful to the gospel and church teaching on the preferential option for the poor, they stood for social justice and peace.

Romero himself had taught that those who died fighting for justice were "martyrs":

> For me those who are true martyrs in the popular sense
> . . . are true men who have gone to dangerous areas,
> where the White Warrior Union threatens, where someone can be pointed out and eventually killed as they
> killed Christ.[22]

Romero himself, in fact, was popularly venerated as a martyr and saint immediately after his death in 1980. Many people came to his tomb to pray and to lay flowers at the Cathedral of the Holy Savior in San Salvador. He was declared a martyr by Pope Francis on February 3, 2015 and canonized as a saint on October 14, 2018.

The situation in Latin America is problematic when declaring someone a martyr because there Christians are killing Christians. A Catholic bishop might be killed by soldiers ordered by officers, perhaps with the permission of the president of the country, all of whom were baptized Catholics! Thomas Aquinas taught that a martyr is simply a Christian killed by enemies trying to destroy the Catholic faith. Liberation theologians have expanded the definition of martyrdom to include those who die while defending the poor against the injustice of the state, because such martyrdom occurs frequently in Latin America.

Leonardo Boff, a Brazilian theologian, views Jesus as the proto-martyr and emphasizes that it is not the suffering and death

21. John Paul II, *Ut Unum Sint*, 84.
22. Quoted in Sobrino, "Our World," 18.

that makes a martyr but the "cause."[23] The gospel teaches: "Blessed are those who are persecuted for righteousness' sake, for theirs is the kingdom of heaven" (Matt 5:10) and "you will be brought before governors and kings for My sake, as a testimony to them and to the Gentiles" (Matt 10:18). Stressing the politically subversive nature of Christianity, Boff holds that early Christians were killed because they threatened the political-religious foundation of the Roman Empire and its leaders. Stretching the concept of martyrdom, Boff thus asserts that modern-day martyrs died for their faith, like Christians in earlier times:

> Not a few Christians . . . because of the Gospel, make a preferential option for the poor, for their liberation, for the defence of their rights. In the name of this option they stand up and denounce the exercise of domination and all forms of social dehumanization. They may be persecuted, arrested, tortured and killed. They, too, are martyrs in the strict sense of the word.[24]

With this supposition, martyrs thus can include Christians who died for their faith in their effort to defend their brothers and sisters from injustice and exploitation.

Jon Sobrino writes that in our time, the situation in Latin America has produced Christians who have died violently not "on account of their witness to faith but because of the compassion that stems from their faith."[25] They are "Jesus martyrs" who suffered violence and death like the Savior. Strictly speaking, they are not those "who *die* for Christ" but "those who die *like* Jesus *for the cause of Jesus*"; they are "martyrs *in* the church but not martyrs *of* the church."[26] These martyrs find their configuration in the life and death of Jesus. They are killed not because of hatred for their faith but rather hatred for their involvement with the lives of the poor and dispossessed, which they carried out in mercy and compassion for God's people.

23. Boff, "Martyrdom," 13.
24. Boff, "Martyrdom," 13.
25. Sobrino, "Our World," 17.
26. Sobrino, "Our World," 19.

These Christians include bishops, priests, sisters, lay workers, peasants, students, lawyers, and journalists. In one way or another they have exposed the unjust structures in society that have caused the suffering and death of many poor people. They are compassionate individuals who have fought against the social, economic, and political elites who were determined to maintain their wealth and privileges at the expense of the poor.

The reality of El Salvador had prompted Romero to preach about the significance of Rutilio Grande's death: "What does the church offer in this universal fight for the liberation from all this misery?"[27] The liberation that the church offers is exemplified by the ministry of Rutilio, working for and with the poor in solidarity against injustice and exploitation. Rutilio died because he was faithful to the social doctrine of the church. Deeply saddened by Rutilio's death, Romero made personal pleas to the perpetrators:

> I want to tell you, criminal brothers, who already are in
> ex-communion with the church, and are listening on the
> radio. . . . I want to tell you, criminal brothers, that we
> love you and we ask God for forgiveness for your hearts,
> because the love of the church is not capable of hating, it
> does not have enemies. The love of the Lord inspired the
> action of Rutilio Grande.[28]

Romero thanked the Society of Jesus for sending men such as Rutilio Grande to El Salvador and "illuminating so many on the roads to Aguilares."[29] The roads to Aguilares symbolize the El Salvador way of the cross, where sufferings and death for justice, peace, and righteousness will lead to the resurrection. Rutilio Grande was the first Salvadoran priest to be killed in the 1970s for political reasons. But he was regarded by many in the country as a martyr for justice.

Willing to sacrifice his life for his fellow Salvadorans, Romero has taught that martyrdom is a grace of God. Should his enemies succeeded in killing him, he would pardon them so that they

27. Quoted in Thiede, *Remembering Oscar Romero*, 41.

28. Quoted in Thiede, *Remembering Oscar Romero*, 42.

29. Quoted in Thiede, *Remembering Oscar Romero*, 42.

would know that they were wasting their time—a bishop will die but the people of God, the church, will never perish. The many martyrs in El Salvador manifest that the church is persecuted for its fidelity to the teaching of Jesus Christ. This sad state of affairs—persecution and martyrdom—is also a glorious witness to the faith of the people in the nation that has the Savior himself as its patron.

Maryknoll Sisters Maura Clarke and Ita Ford, Maryknoll lay missionary Jean Donovan, and Ursuline Sister Dorothy Kazel from the United States were raped, tortured, and killed on December 2, 1980, in the same year Romero was murdered. And yet, the United States continued to support the military government in El Salvador throughout the 1980s. On December 11, 1981, an armed battalion executed more than eight hundred civilians in a village called El Mozote; this event is now referred to as the El Mozote Massacre.[30]

The right-wing Arena Party led by Roberto D'Aubuisson came into power in El Salvador after the 1989 election, in the same year that six Jesuit priests and their helpers were killed by the army on the campus of UCA. The death of these priests and religious represents a tiny fraction of the more than eighty thousand Salvadorans killed by the government-backed death squads since 1979.[31] Their victims were people working in both religious and secular organizations demanding land reform and better working conditions for the poor. We can consider these victims "anonymous martyrs" because they died fighting for the kingdom of God.

## Justice and Peace

Romero was also convinced that peace and non-violence could only be achieved when there is justice. In other words, violence is a product of unjust economic and social structures in society, which the bishops at Medellín characterized as institutional violence. This institutionalized violence or legalized violence comes

---

30. Teaching Central America, "History of El Salvador," para. 25.
31. Teaching Central America, "History of El Salvador," para. 27.

in the form of economic exploitation, political domination, or the military's violation of human rights. The fact is "violence starts with the structures of violence."[32]

In El Salvador, when people started to organize themselves to dismantle those structures of violence, the elites would retaliate with further violence with the help of the government-backed military. The wealthy class would do all they could to stop any revolutionary change that threatened their lifestyle—the "privileged few repressed the ones seeking change, so this violence of oppression became a violence of repression."[33] Many of the oppressed believed the only way to bring about change was through the violence of revolution. But Ignacio Ellacuría insisted that the solution is to struggle against the first violence so as to prevent the violence of repression and revolutionary violence through negotiation, dialogue, and reconciliation.

While the church permits a "legitimate defense" as a means to uphold human rights, it fervently promotes non-violence, which is based on the Gospel teaching of turning the other cheek to an aggressor. Not simply a passive response, this turning the other cheek to the aggressor requires moral strength and the conviction that peace is more powerful than violence. Unfortunately in El Salvador, there existed fanatical groups who believed in "divinizing violence as the only source of justice."[34] But with or without such responses, violence is not going to stop if there is vast economic disparity between the rich and the poor. There is no justice and peace if widespread poverty prevails.

Back in 1967, Pope Paul VI wrote an encyclical letter entitled *Populorum Progressio* (On the Development of Peoples) where he lamented "in certain regions a privileged minority enjoys the refinements of life, while the rest of the inhabitants, impoverished and disunited, 'are deprived of almost all possibility of acting on their own initiative and responsibility, and often subsist in living

---

32. Gumbleton, "If You Want Peace, Work for Justice," 38.

33. Gumbleton, "If You Want Peace, Work for Justice," 38.

34. Brockman, *Romero*, 143–44.

and working conditions unworthy of the human person."[35] Most wealthy faithful do not see structural injustice, nor do they feel obligated to reach out to those who are in need.

In 1971, Pope Paul VI called a synod of bishops and produced a document entitled *Justice in the World*. This synod was of historical importance as it put the church squarely on the side of those who fight against injustice, on the side of the poor, oppressed, and voiceless. The synod placed the theme of social justice and concern at the center of the church's life. The document acknowledges the concept of structural or institutionalized injustice in society. Liberation in Christ includes all aspects of life and not merely inner spiritual transformation. Education is not just learning traditional values but "conscientization and criticism of structures, standards and values obtaining in various societies"; moreover, "social reform has been firmly included as an essential element of the pastoral ministry at all levels."[36] Structural social injustice occurs when the community at the national or international level is organized in such a way that it works to the detriment of some individuals or groups and to the favor of others in that society.

John Paul II, too, highlighted how our social mechanisms can lead to poverty, which is the thrust of his teaching on structural sin: "social, economic, and political structures, which are frequently agents of violence and injustice."[37] This means no peace, no justice. Today, we have 20 percent of the world's population living in abject poverty, 60 percent in some degree of poverty, and the remaining 20 percent enjoying 87 percent of the earth's resources and wealth. This happens not because those living in the northern hemisphere are more intelligent or work harder than the poor people in other parts of the planet. It is because they have manipulated the economic order, the structures and systems of society, solely to their advantage and benefit.

According to Gustavo Gutiérrez, poverty is the result of how we have organized our society, not only the way we distribute our

35. Pope Paul VI, *Populorum Progressio*, 9.

36. Darring, "1971 Synod of Bishops."

37. Christiansen, "Catholic Peacemaking, 1991–2005."

resources, but the way we think about and classify racial, cultural, and gender issues. Poverty has many aspects, including economic, cultural, racial, social and gender-related facets. We now understand that poverty is not destined; it is human-made, a misfortune produced by injustice, which can be avoided. Theologically speaking, the root of poverty is injustice, which is the refusal to love. The core of our Christian faith is love, and thus refusal to love is sin.[38] This fundamental virtue of charity is exemplified in the life and death of Óscar Romero.

38. Gutiérrez, "Liberation Theology for the Twenty-First Century," 50.

Chapter 4

# The Cave and the Cathedral in
# *Death Comes for the Archbishop*

WILLA CATHER (1873–1947) WAS an American novelist renowned
for depicting the settlers and frontier life on the American plains.
Her upbringing in Nebraska and her experiences with the immi-
grant communities there greatly influenced her writing. Cather's
family relocated to frontier Nebraska when she was nine years old,
and she settled in the village of Red Cloud at the age of ten. Growing up in this environment, she was surrounded by European im-
migrants, including Swedes, Bohemians, Russians, and Germans,
who were working to cultivate the Great Plains.[1]

Cather's talent for journalism and storytelling became apparent when she studied at the University of Nebraska. After
graduating in 1895, she secured a position at a family magazine in
Pittsburgh, Pennsylvania. She later worked as a music, drama, and
copyeditor for the *Pittsburgh Leader*. In 1901, she started teaching
while continuing to pursue her writing career. In 1903, she published her first book of verse, entitled *April Twilights*. Two years
later, in 1905, she released her first collection of short stories, *The*

---

1. *Encyclopedia Britannica Online*, s.v. "Willa Cather," https://www.britan-
nica.com/biography/Willa-Cather.

*Troll Garden.* Her success in the literary world led to her appointment as the managing editor of *McClure's Magazine.*[2]

One of Cather's best-known novels is *Death Comes for the Archbishop* (1927). Her main characters, Jean Latour and Joseph Vaillant, are closely based on the historical Jean-Baptiste Lamy, the first archbishop of Santa Fe, and his vicar-general, Machebeuf, recorded in Father William Howlett's, *The Life of the Right Reverend Joseph P. Machebeuf.* Written in a lyrical and evocative style, Cather pays meticulous attention to details, vividly describing the landscapes and cultural practices of the Southwest. Her narration is deeply introspective, intuitively engaging the reader with the feelings and thinking of the characters.

This chapter attempts to explore her portrayal of priests, focusing on the transformation of the protagonist, Bishop Jean Latour, from an ambitious church leader to a compassionate priest capable of accepting the simple faith of the Mexicans and the spiritual tradition of the Indians. While his encounter with native spirituality is embodied in his experience in a ceremonial cave, his ambition is epitomized by the construction of a cathedral. As he sheds his European sense of cultural superiority, Latour begins to accept and appreciate the local traditions as he labors to establish his diocese in New Mexico. Ironically, the transformative learning process takes place in his moments of depression, self-doubt, and disillusionment. The novel opens with an opulent setting in the Eternal City, "in the gardens of a villa in the Sabine Hills, overlooking Rome."[3] It presents a marked contrast to the southwestern frontier of the United States where Latour labors.

## Prologue: At Rome

During a lavish dinner in Rome, three cardinals and one missionary bishop appoint the French priest Jean Marie Latour to revive the mission in New Mexico. According to the bishop, the church,

2. *Encyclopedia Britannica Online,* s.v. "Willa Cather,"
3. Cather, *Death Comes for the Archbishop,* 3.

started by the Franciscan friars in the sixteenth century, is now falling into ruin due to few priests who are "without guidance and discipline."[4] The four European clerics regard the people of New Mexico as backward and disunited: "Some thirty Indian nations . . . each with its own customs and language, many of them fiercely hostile to each other. And the Mexicans, a naturally devout people, untaught and unshepherded, they cling to the faith of their fathers."[5]

Thus, the priest chosen for the mission must be capable of dealing with rather ignorant people, corrupt clergy, and local politics. The host, a Spanish cardinal named García María de Allande, asserts, "The new vicar must be a young man, of strong constitution, full of zeal, and, above all, intelligent. He will have to deal with savagery and ignorance, with dissolute priests and political intrigue. He must be a man to whom *order* is necessary—as dear as life."[6] After this brief but significant prologue, the story shifts to Latour's life in central New Mexico.

## Colonialism and Imperialism

The story is set in the Southwest with its legacy of Spanish colonialism and the presence of American imperialism. The Spaniards established the Catholic Church in New Mexico in the seventeenth century, but an Indian uprising in 1680 drove them out. The only successful insurrection against colonialism in North America was a revolution against Spanish religious, economic, and political domination of the Pueblos.[7] However, without much supervision from Rome, the church in New Mexico developed its syncretic ways.

Bishop Latour's effort to reassert church authority in New Mexico coincides with the time when the "Yankee traders" and

4. Cather, *Death Comes for the Archbishop*, 7.
5. Cather, *Death Comes for the Archbishop*, 7.
6. Cather, *Death Comes for the Archbishop*, 8.
7. Indian Pueblo Cultural Center, "Brief History of the Pueblo Revolt."

soldiers dominated the territory, which had been taken by force. Mostly Protestant, many of these Americans were hostile to the Mexicans, who were predominantly Catholic. Although Latour scorns the crass culture of the Americans, he attempts to maintain cordial relations with them. In a letter, he writes to his brother:

> All day I am an American in speech and thought—yes, in heart, too. The kindness of the American traders, and especially of the military officers at the Fort, commands more than a superficial loyalty. I mean to help the officers at their task here. I can assist them more than they realize. The Church can do more than the Fort to make these poor Mexicans "good Americans." And it is for the people's good; there is no other way in which they can better their condition.[8]

Latour understands the need for the Catholic mission to accommodate and work within the confines of American expansionist policy and Protestant culture. This strategy would also improve the living conditions of the Mexicans. Thus, when Sada, a Mexican woman enslaved by an American Protestant family, sneaks into his church to pray, Latour does not encourage her to escape again. He is afraid to antagonize those "low caste Protestants who took every occasion to make trouble for the Catholics."[9] Like most Europeans, he believes that native culture is primitive and inferior, and that assimilation to Western ways will benefit them.

As a priest, Latour understands his role primarily as administering the sacraments to the Mexican people, who have been without worthy priests for a long time; the only priests present are corrupt and lazy. In spite of their sincere piety, Latour considers that the faith of the Mexicans is immature and superstitious. In dealing with them, he "repeatedly demonstrates a detached, analytical, and, at times, condescending stance when engaging with the spirituality of Mexican Catholics."[10] Latour sees himself as the one who will revive and inspire the believers; he reflects, "The

8. Cather, *Death Comes for the Archbishop*, 35–36.

9. Cather, *Death Comes for the Archbishop*, 216.

10. Old, "Making Good Americans," 55.

Faith planted by the Spanish friars and watered with their blood was not dead; it awaited only the toil of the husbandman."[11] Latour believes Christianity is not dead in New Mexico, but it needs a European priest like him to guide the faithful towards greater fidelity to the church. However, to do this successfully, the bishop must overcome the social and cultural rifts between him and the people to whom he is ministering.

## The Cave: Stone Lips

During a fierce storm, Latour's guide, Jacinto, takes him into a cave called Stone Lips, a sacred spot for native rituals. Jacinto speaks about Indian religious ceremonies in this spot, which makes Latour uncomfortable, "Great as was his need of shelter, the Bishop on his way down the ladder was struck by a reluctance, an extreme distaste for the place. The air in the cave was glacial, penetrated to the very bones, and he detected at once a fetid odour, not very strong but highly disagreeable."[12] After carefully examining the place, Jacinto confesses his reluctance to bring the Catholic priest there, saying, "Padre . . . I do not know if it was right to bring you here. This place is used by my people for ceremonies and is known only to us. When you go out from here you must forget." Latour replies, "I will forget, certainly. But unless we can have a fire, we had better go back into the storm. I feel ill here already."[13]

After Jacinto has closed the hole in the cavern wall, he begins to light a fire, and "the odour so disagreeable to the Bishop soon vanished . . . but the dizzy noise in Father Latour's head persisted."[14] As he begins to feel warm and comfortable, "he perceived an extraordinary vibration in this cavern; it hummed like a hive of bees,

11. Cather, *Death Comes for the Archbishop*, 32.

12. Cather, *Death Comes for the Archbishop*, 127.

13. Cather, *Death Comes for the Archbishop*, 128.

14. Cather, *Death Comes for the Archbishop*, 129.

like a heavy roll of distant drums."[15] Jacinto then leads the bishop
to listen at a fissure in the stone floor:

> He [Latour] told himself that he was listening to one of
> the oldest voices of the earth. What he heard was the
> sound of a great underground river, flowing through a
> resounding cavern. The water was far, far below, perhaps
> as deep as the foot of the mountain, a flood moving in ut-
> ter blackness under ribs of antediluvian rock. It was not
> a rushing noise, but the sound of a great flood moving
> with majesty and power.[16]

When awakened, the bishop secretly observes Jacinto performing a ritual unknown to him: "there against the wall was his
guide, standing on some invisible foothold, his arms outstretched
against the rock, his body flattened against it, his ear over that
patch of fresh mud, listening, listening with supersensual ear, it
seemed, and he looked to be supported against the rock by the intensity of his solicitude."[17] The bishop closes his eyes quietly. Later
when they reached home, "he still felt a certain curiosity about
this ceremonial cave, and Jacinto's puzzling behaviour."[18] Latour
realizes that neither the white men nor the Mexicans can fathom
the minds of the Indians regarding their beliefs.

What takes place in that cave is a mystery for Westerners,
even though there were stories regarding the ceremonies. Later,
Latour asks a trader, Zeb Orchard, about a report of a snake being kept in the cave. Orchard replies, "They do keep some sort of
varmint out in the mountain, that they bring in for their religious
ceremonies. . . . But I don't know if it's a snake or not. No white
man knows anything about Indian religion, padre."[19] One may
wonder why Latour does not ask the locals about Indian religious
practices but seeks the opinion of another white man.

---

15. Cather, *Death Comes for the Archbishop*, 129.
16. Cather, *Death Comes for the Archbishop*, 130.
17. Cather, *Death Comes for the Archbishop*, 131–32.
18. Cather, *Death Comes for the Archbishop*, 133.
19. Cather, *Death Comes for the Archbishop*, 134.

Latour admits that he admires the Indian sense of religiosity and their reverence for customs and traditions, which also play an important part in his religion. The trader also remarks that Indians are good Catholics but will never relinquish their traditional beliefs entirely. The local shamans have their mysteries, but Orchard is not sure what is real and what is not. While Latour acknowledges the natives' spiritual sensitivities, an alternative form of religious belief and practices alarms him. In fact, the realization that the cave saved his life makes him apprehensive. It is in his emptiness and suffering that Latour begins to experience the consolation of folk piety.

## Depression and Doubt

As time passes, discouraged by the lack of success of his mission, Latour begins to experience depression and doubt. While the Mexican Catholics resist his authority, the Indians are indifferent towards Christianity. Failing to improve the spiritual and material life of the faithful in the diocese leads to despair: "His prayers were empty words and brought him no refreshment. His soul had become a barren field. He had nothing within himself to give his priests or his people. His work seemed superficial, a house built upon the sands. His great diocese was still a heathen country."[20] Unable to evangelize effectively among both the Mexicans and the Indians, Latour believes himself to be a failure. In this moment of anguish, Latour unexpectedly encounters someone who restores his faith and inspires him to persevere in his mission.

On a cold winter night, Latour meets Sada, an elderly Mexican woman taking refuge in his church. A slave of an American Protestant family, the Smiths, Sada is not allowed to attend Mass or receive visits from a priest. Treated badly and not even permitted to sleep in the heated room of the house, she went to "the House of God to pray."[21] The bishop is accustomed to bestowing gifts on his

20. Cather, *Death Comes for the Archbishop*, 211.
21. Cather, *Death Comes for the Archbishop*, 213.

faithful, but now he is receiving a gift from Sada, "He received the miracle in her heart into his own, saw through her eyes, knew that his poverty was as bleak as hers. . . . This church was Sada's house, and he was a servant in it."[22]

When praying beside Sada, Latour experiences the profound presence of God. As he tells Fr. Vaillant:

> Never . . . had it been permitted him to behold such deep experience of the holy joy of religion as on that pale December night. He was able to feel, kneeling beside her, the preciousness of the things of the altar to her who was without possessions; the tapers, the image of the Virgin, the figures of the saints, the Cross that took away indignity from suffering and made pain and poverty a means of fellowship with Christ.[23]

"Not often, indeed, had Jean Marie Latour come so near to the Fountain of all Pity as in the Lady Chapel that night."[24] Cather's use of his full Christian name suggests that Latour is not just Sada's bishop but her brother as well, without distinction of class, ethnicity, or gender. Latour's humility is revealed by his openness to receive the gift of faith from an enslaved Mexican. Just as Latour has much to offer to the Mexicans and Indians, now he recognizes that they, too, have as much to offer to him as well. This encounter with the poor and marginalized is indeed a moment of grace and transformation for the bishop. Now Latour understands that the strangeness of Mexican piety, different from his French faith, is God's gift to him. Understanding and appreciating the sincere devotion of the poor also leads Latour to recognize the integrity of other religious beliefs, as we shall see in his relationship with the Navajo Eusabio.

22. Cather, *Death Comes for the Archbishop*, 218.
23. Cather, *Death Comes for the Archbishop*, 217.
24. Cather, *Death Comes for the Archbishop*, 217.

## Expression of Religious Gravity

Friendship with the Navajo Eusabio, whom he highly regards, makes Latour appreciate native culture. His regular visits to Eusabio's home demonstrate his acceptance of not just their local hospitality but also his respect for their religious beliefs. While he does not understand the Navajo language, he enjoys their dancing and singing, which he recognizes as an "expression of religious gravity."[25] On the way back to Santa Fe, the bishop observes Eusabio's deep reverence for the land and realizes that the native sense of the sacred is different from Christian understanding:

> They seemed to have none of the European's desires to "master" nature, to arrange and re-create. They spend their ingenuity in the other direction; in accommodating themselves to the scene in which they found themselves. This was not so much from indolence, the Bishop thought, as from an inherited caution and respect. It was as if the great country were asleep. And they wished to carry on their lives without awakening it; or as if the spirits of earth and air and water were things not to antagonize and arouse.[26]

Given our present-day environmental crisis, we appreciate Cather's portrayal of the wisdom of native Indians, their tradition of conservation, and their sense of stewardship towards the land and all living things. When the Indians at Ácoma were afraid to develop the land, Latour thought they were lazy or superstitious. To the contrary, their respect and reverence for nature forewarns them to be cautious when dealing with their land.

While Latour may not have succeeded in converting the Indians to Christianity, he won their hearts. He understands that "the Mexicans were always Mexicans, the Indians were always Indians."[27] In other words, they are rooted in their distinct ways of life, just as he is rooted in French tradition. Eventually, the bishop

---

25. Cather, *Death Comes for the Archbishop*, 231.
26. Cather, *Death Comes for the Archbishop*, 234.
27. Cather, *Death Comes for the Archbishop*, 286.

comes to identify with the diverse cultures of New Mexico. His friendship with the Indians is not based on a common faith but on respect for their way of life. Canyon de Chelly was the Navajo ancestral home, "Their gods were there, just as the Padre's God was in his church."[28] Knowing that most Navajos will never accept Christianity, Latour believes that God's grace will still reach them in some way because "the expulsion of the Navajos from their country, which had been theirs no man knew how long, had seemed to him an injustice that cried to Heaven."[29] Bishop Latour believes that God will not allow this tribe to perish.

## The Good, the Bad, and the Ugly

Latour is described as a gentle person, even as he proceeds to create "order" among the people in the territory: "Everything showed him to be a man of gentle birth—brave, sensitive, courteous. His manners, even when he was alone in the desert, were distinguished. He had a kind of courtesy toward himself, toward his beasts, toward the juniper tree, before which he knelt, and the God whom he was addressing."[30] A man in constant contact with God, "his devotions lasted perhaps half an hour, and when he rose he looked refreshed."[31] While Latour is a refined gentleman, well-educated and thoughtful, Joseph Vaillant, his vicar, who is described as "ugly" and "holy,"[32] is more practical and outgoing. They complement each other in their mission work. Friends since their childhood days, both priests overcome the corruption of the Spanish friars, natural disasters, the harshness of the desert landscape, and the hostility of the Hopi and Navajo natives as they labor to establish the church in the frontier.

---

28. Cather, *Death Comes for the Archbishop*, 295.

29. Cather, *Death Comes for the Archbishop*, 292.

30. Cather, *Death Comes for the Archbishop*, 19.

31. Cather, *Death Comes for the Archbishop*, 19.

32. Cather, *Death Comes for the Archbishop*, 56.

In contrast to the good priests, as shown in the sacrificial spirit of Latour and Vaillant, Cather introduces some bad priests, such as the self-indulgent Padre Gallegos, "a great gambler."[33] She writes, "Though Padre Gallegos was ten years older than the Bishop, he would still dance the fandango five nights running, as if he could never have enough of it. He had many friends in the American colony, with whom he played poker and went hunting, when he was not dancing with the Mexicans."[34] Further, unlike Latour, Gallegos was not interested in going out for the mission because "he had no liking for scanty food and a bed on the rocks."[35]

Padre Jesus de Baca, in contrast to Gallegos, appears to be a better pastor; he is "an old white-haired man, almost blind, who had been at Isleta many years and had won the confidence and affection of his Indians."[36] His dwelling reveals his austerity, which pleases the bishop: "The priest's house was white within and without, like all the Isleta houses, and was almost as bare as an Indian dwelling. The old man was poor, and too soft-hearted to press the pueblo people for pesos. An Indian girl cooked his beans and cornmeal mush for him; he required little else."[37] In fact, Padre Jesus "was simple almost to childishness, and very superstitious. But there was a quality of golden goodness about him."[38]

## The Legend of Fray Baltazar

The most dramatic description of a depraved cleric is Fray Baltazar, who is as ambitious as the Spanish Fathers and decadent as Gallegos. Cather names this section "The Legend of Fray Baltazar," which suggests a folk tale to be told to future generations. In this episode, Cather gives an example of how a group seeks justice by

33. Cather, *Death Comes for the Archbishop*, 59.
34. Cather, *Death Comes for the Archbishop*, 82.
35. Cather, *Death Comes for the Archbishop*, 83.
36. Cather, *Death Comes for the Archbishop*, 84.
37. Cather, *Death Comes for the Archbishop*, 85.
38. Cather, *Death Comes for the Archbishop*, 86.

participating in a cycle of violence between the oppressed and the oppressor. A priest tells this story at Isleta regarding a tyrannical friar who lives in Àcoma, a city set on a mesa or flat rock. Friar Baltazar oppresses the natives, requiring them to serve him with their best produce. Despised by the people, he forces them to work for him: "Baltazar's tyranny grew little by little, and the Ácoma people were sometimes at the point of revolt."[39]

One evening Baltazar throws a dinner party with fine food for some priests. One of the servants, a young boy, accidentally spills some gravy on one of the priests sitting at the table. Furious, Baltazar throws an empty pewter mug at the "clumsy lad with malediction," killing him instantly.[40] His guest priests flee at once, leaving him alone. He goes to the kitchen and "took the turkey from the spit, not because he felt any inclination for food, but from an instinct of compassion, quite as if the bird could suffer from being burned to a crisp."[41] The shocking contradiction between showing compassion for a dead bird and disregarding the life of a young native boy reveals the degeneracy of Baltazar.

Taking the law into their own hands, the townspeople enter Baltazar's house, carry him out and fling him over the mesa's edge to his death. An abusive and violent priest, Baltazar gets punished through this rough justice. In a broader perspective, this episode reveals the tension between the natives and the foreign missionary. The narrator regards this tale as a legend, giving it a "mythic dimension"—a warning and a guide to social norms.[42]

Renegade priests in this novel include Padre José Antonio Martinez and Padre Marino Lucero. They have a love-hate relationship as they like to argue and tell stories about each other but remain friends till the end. Martinez has instigated an Indian uprising against the Americans. While seven of the Taos Indians were tried before a military court and hung for the massacre, Martinez was not called upon to account for the plot. In fact, he "managed to

39. Cather, *Death Comes for the Archbishop*, 107.
40. Cather, *Death Comes for the Archbishop*, 110.
41. Cather, *Death Comes for the Archbishop*, 111.
42. Bayley, "Conflict of Legends," 840.

profit considerably by the affair."[43] A despot, Martinez's "mouth was the very assertion of violent, uncurbed passions and tyrannical self-will; the full lips thrust out and taut, like the flesh of animals distended by fear or desire."[44] Convinced that celibacy was against nature, Martinez violated a young woman who wanted to enter religious life.

Like Martinez, Lucero loves to have power and authority. Lucero proudly proclaims, "Avarice . . . was the one passion that grew stronger and sweeter in old age."[45] Lucero loves money just as Martinez loves women. When Lucero dies, he leaves a great deal of money: "A great sum for one old priest to have scraped together in a country parish down at the bottom of a ditch."[46] That these men are still very much alive in the novel suggests the presence of self-indulgent priests up to this day. Each personified a particular vice: "Baltazar addicted to pleasures of the table, Martinez to pleasures of the bed, and Lucero to pleasures of the purse."[47]

Trinidad, the nephew of Lucero, is supposed to be trained by Martinez for the priesthood, but the young man is treated more like "a poor relation or servant" by the priest.[48] The "ugly" appearance of Trinidad repels Latour:

> Father Latour disliked his personality so much that he could scarcely look at him. His fat face was irritatingly stupid, and had the grey, oily look of soft cheeses. . . . [H]e said not one word during supper but ate as if he were afraid of never seeing food again. When his attention left his plate for a moment, it was fixed in the same greedy way upon the girl who served the table—and who seemed to regard him with careless contempt.[49]

43. Cather, *Death Comes for the Archbishop*, 140.
44. Cather, *Death Comes for the Archbishop*, 141.
45. Cather, *Death Comes for the Archbishop*, 161.
46. Cather, *Death Comes for the Archbishop*, 172.
47. Dinn, "Novelist's Miracle," 41.
48. Cather, *Death Comes for the Archbishop*, 145.
49. Cather, *Death Comes for the Archbishop*, 145.

Trinidad embodies the dissolute nature of Martinez himself and his household, and it is no wonder that Latour finds him rather disgusting. But the bishop is not without his own faults.

## Romanesque Cathedral

Latour doubts the sincerity of the early missionary priest who built Ácoma, the "fortress-like" church on the mesa: "The more Father Latour examined this church, the more he was inclined to think that Fray Ramirez, or some Spanish priest who followed him, was not altogether innocent of worldly ambition, and that they built for their own satisfaction, perhaps, rather than according to the needs of the Indians."[50] However, Latour is also not entirely innocent of those accusations when he decides to build a Romanesque cathedral in Santa Fe:

> Bishop Latour had one very keen worldly ambition—to build in Santa Fé a cathedral which would be worthy of a setting naturally beautiful. As he cherished this wish and meditated upon it, he came to feel that such a building might be a continuation of himself and his purpose, a physical body full of his aspirations after he had passed from the scene.[51]

The cathedral's construction, an edifice built in Western architectural style, is also unrelated to the needs and preferences of the local people. It is the hope of Latour that this cathedral will prolong his legacy, becoming a legendary structure. As he says to Fr. Joseph, "Perhaps, after all, something would remain through the years to come: some ideal, or memory, or legend."[52] Latour's desire to build this church, a Romanesque cathedral, as a symbol of Christian values betrays Western domination, expanding European influence through architecture and transforming the landscape to something closer to his homeland.

50. Cather, *Death Comes for the Archbishop*, 101.
51. Cather, *Death Comes for the Archbishop*, 175.
52. Cather, *Death Comes for the Archbishop*, 254.

This ambition of Latour reveals his colonial mindset, bent on promoting his agenda and ignoring the wishes and needs of the natives to whom he is ministering.

It is no wonder that Vaillant, a more practical priest, feels uneasy about the whole project. He says, "I had no idea you were going in for fine building, when everything about us is so poor—and we ourselves are so poor."[53] Since Latour is his superior, Vaillant is not able to challenge him forthrightly; besides, "constructing one's own history is a sensitive subject, especially when it concerns a white man's attempt to outlive death through a (false, and ultimately bankrupt) memorialization."[54] Constructing a cathedral in the French style in Santa Fe reveals Latour's deep-seated desire to immortalize himself and his work. Regarding this episode, Nina Baym comments that "white people resist death while Native people accept it within the flow of nature."[55] In the erection of this edifice, Latour hopes to prolong his legacy.

Once the cathedral is built, the narrator questions the appropriateness and relevance of the structure: "No one but Molny [the French architect who builds the cathedral] and the Bishop had ever seemed to enjoy the beautiful site of that building—perhaps no one ever would."[56] Molny tells Latour, "Setting is accident. Either a building is a part of a place, or it is not. Once that kinship is there, time will only make it stronger."[57] Without consulting the local people, the archbishop has built a cathedral that seems out of place in terms of its architectural style and function. For whom was the cathedral constructed and for what purpose? Obviously, it is to satisfy Latour's desire and need to immortalize himself.

Everything that the cathedral stands for may not be part of the setting. If it is not incorporated into the setting or surroundings, no one will appreciate it, and it will not become a legend. In fact, at the end of his life, Latour feels sad that he is not able

53. Cather, *Death Comes for the Archbishop*, 244.
54. Bayley, "Conflict of Legends," 838.
55. Baym, *Women Writers of the American West*, 245.
56. Cather, *Death Comes for the Archbishop*, 271.
57. Cather, *Death Comes for the Archbishop*, 272.

to record in writing the legends and customs of the past: "Those truths and fancies relating to a bygone time would probably be lost; the old legends and customs and superstitions were already dying out."[58] Here, the narrator questions which tradition, including Latour's cathedral, will acquire a legendary status.[59]

## "Cather has given us an American Saint"[60]

While we have witnessed the saintliness of Latour, he is not without his shortcomings. He is a man who stands out among his peers but remains fallibly human; he has both strengths and weaknesses. Latour admits his selfish motive when he recalls his friend, Fr. Joseph Vaillant, back to Santa Fe: "I sent for you because I felt the need of your companionship. I used my authority as a Bishop to gratify my personal wish."[61] Fr. Joseph's frequent absence worries Latour due to his covetous nature and unhealthy attachment. In his final days, the archbishop envies the early Christians, whom he thinks had a much easier life, even if they suffered: "it all happened in that safe little Mediterranean world, amid the old manners, the old landmarks. If they endured martyrdom, they died among their brethren, their relics were piously preserved, their names lived in the mouths of holy men."[62] Be that as it may, Latour has the courage and humility to admit his flaws.

Latour asserts that he has witnessed the end of black slavery and the restoration of Navajo land, but in reality, the two great wrongs were not "quite" righted. Besides, Latour is also part of the Catholic Church expansionism that seeks to dominate the cultural and religious life of the natives. Latour's fascination with the miracle stories of the missionary Junipero Serra (1713–84) reveals that he is blind to abuses and atrocities committed by missionaries

58. Cather, *Death Comes for the Archbishop*, 277.

59. Bayley, "Conflict of Legends," 841.

60. Bohlke, "Willa Cather's Nebraska Priests," 264.

61. Cather, *Death Comes for the Archbishop*, 253. For a detailed account of Latour's flaws, see Shaw, "Women and the Father," 62–65.

62. Cather, *Death Comes for the Archbishop*, 278.

when they attempted to evangelize the natives in California, Texas, Arizona, and New Mexico.[63] He appears to have tolerated and accepted slavery in that he does not encourage Sada to escape, as we have seen.

When he first arrived in New Mexico to establish a diocese, Bishop Latour believed that Roman Catholicism would have a civilizing influence on the native population. But when the mission falls short of his expectations, he experiences a crisis of faith and despondency, which forces him to reconsider his role as shepherd of the flock. As he approaches the end of his life, gaining spiritual insight, Latour begins to understand the church as communion and solidarity with people of different beliefs and cultural backgrounds.[64] This is demonstrated by the many people from all walks of life mourning him when he passed on. Cather writes:

> When the Cathedral bell tolled just after dark, the Mexican population of Santa Fe fell upon their knees, and all American Catholics as well. Many others who did not kneel prayed in their hearts. Eusabio and the Tesuque boys went quietly away to tell their people; and the next morning the old Archbishop lay before the high altar in the church he had built.[65]

Thus, people from diverse cultural and religious backgrounds pray for the archbishop of New Mexico at his passing. Mexican and American Catholics, Protestants, Navajo and Tesuque Indians, all remember him in their own ways, as he is laid to rest in a French Romanesque cathedral in Santa Fe.

63. Sevick, "Catholic Expansionism," 196.
64. Old, "Making Good Americans," 54.
65. Cather, *Death Comes for the Archbishop*, 299.

## Chapter 5

# Tears of a True Priest
# in *The Diary of a Country Priest*

GEORGE BERNANOS (1888–1948) IS relatively unknown in the English-speaking world, but in France and throughout Europe his novels and social-cum-political essays were widely read during his lifetime. His works on religious and philosophical themes still command great interest among discerning readers. Born in Paris on February 20, 1888, he was raised in a middle-class devout Roman Catholic home. During his formative years, France was a deeply divided nation, culturally and spiritually. Although Paris was an international city attracting artists and writers from all over the world, millions of French citizens, especially those living in rural areas, were still very conservative and religious. A devout Catholic, the young Bernanos was deeply distrustful of progressive and liberal movements that campaigned for social, cultural, and political reforms.

Educated by the Jesuits, Bernanos studied law and literature. He joined the conservative Action Française movement headed by Charles Maurras and Léon Daudet. Before World War I, he edited the Royalist *L'Avant garde de Normandie* weekly. During the war, he fought in the French army, was wounded, and was subsequently decorated. In 1917, he married Jeanne Talbert d'Arc, and they had

72

six children. In response to his interest in writing, he made a decisive break with Action Française. Conscious of the poverty and injustice prevalent in France in the 1920s and 1930s, Bernanos was critical of his beloved Catholic Church for its complicity with France's rich and powerful.

Bernanos's early career involved working for an insurance company, which required him to travel frequently. During his travels, he keenly observed people and situations, taking notes that would later inform his writing. Despite a demanding job, he had a deep-seated desire to write and pursued various forms of writing, such as stories, novels, and literary essays. By the early 1930s, Bernanos had gained modest recognition for his early novels, including *L'Imposture* and *La Joie*. In addition to his fiction, he also contributed regularly to the newspaper *Le Figaro*. As a thoughtful conservative writer, he possessed a strong Christian conscience, which often influenced his perspectives.

Be that as it may, Bernanos exhibited a complex relationship with the church and political institutions. While he respected them to some extent, he also displayed an intense independence of thought and contempt for worldly powers. He aligned himself with the prophetic tradition of the Old Testament and the teachings of Jesus, which often criticized such powers. Therefore, his literary contributions and his exploration of faith, politics, and social criticism have made him a significant figure in French literature.[1]

Bernanos's literary style is marked by its poetic and philosophical depth, employing rich imagery and symbolism to engage readers. His protagonists are often troubled individuals wrestling with the complexities of the human condition. In narrating the spiritual struggle of an individual, Bernanos's writing is aided by the anti-bourgeois tradition of French literature and the ethos of Catholicism, which portrays evil not "in passionate crimes but in narrow and recalcitrant self-centeredness."[2]

*The Diary of a Country Priest* (*Journal d'un curé de campagne*), published in 1936, is Bernanos's most renowned work. The novel

1. Coles, "Pilgrimage of George Bernanos."
2. Lye, "*Diary of a Country Priest*," 22.

resonated with readers from various backgrounds and nationalities due to its exploration of human experiences and questions of faith, suffering, and redemption. Translated into numerous languages, *The Diary of a Country Priest* allows readers to engage with and reflect on its profound themes. Its enduring popularity, with continued interest among readers, reflect the timeless and universal qualities of Bernanos's storytelling and his ability to touch the hearts and minds of the audience.

## The Diary of a Country Priest

Written in the form of a diary, the novel enables readers to experience the suffering and pain of the priest whose health deteriorates as the narrative progresses. The priest's spiritual journey is interwoven with stories of the people he encounters. The chronicles reveal his relationships with parishioners and his challenges in trying to be a good pastor. Faced with various moral dilemmas, he empathizes with the sufferings and pains of his flock. Introspective and lyrical in its narrative style, the text explores the themes of grace, redemption, and the difficulties of human relationships. The diary forces the priest to be attentive to his daily routine even though he prefers to ignore it. He writes, "I don't think I am doing wrong in jotting down, day by day, without hiding anything, the very simple trivial secrets of a very ordinary kind of life."[3] Yet as his readers would attest, his life is anything but "ordinary."

The book's success led to its adaptation into a film directed by Robert Bresson in 1960, further cementing Bernanos's status as a distinguished figure. George Bernanos passed away on July 5, 1948, in Neuilly-sur-Seine, France, but his literary legacy endures. His exploration of profound themes and his unique literary style continue to captivate readers, ensuring his ongoing significance in French literature.

This chapter explores the protagonist's character development as he evolves from a naive and idealistic young priest to a mature

3. Bernanos, *Diary of a Country Priest*, 7.

74

and compassionate pastor through his encounters with the various people in the rural community. Enduring physical, emotional, and spiritual struggles serves to deepen the priest's love for others. Through his suffering, he experiences grace in his own life as well as in the lives of those under his care. Despite his failures, he is a true priest, one who weeps for his parishioners, and especially for the countess, winning her back to God with his tears. Focusing on the relationship with his mentor, the curé of Torcy, this chapter also discusses the redemptive power of childlike innocence and simplicity.

## The True Priest

According to the protagonist, the true priest is one who has accepted, once and for all, the "terrifying presence" of God in his life.[4] Arriving in Ambricourt with a "soaring love" for his flock, he wants his parish to be a "living cell" of the mystical body of Christ.[5] Ministering to an indifferent and even hostile parish, he soon begins to suffer physical pain and spiritual desolation, thinking that God has abandoned him. At times, he expresses doubt and experiences a crisis of faith. He wonders if his concern for mundane affairs is due to his loss of faith. In spite of his suffering and doubt, he perseveres:

> No, I have not lost my faith. The cruelty of this test, its devastation, like a thunderbolt, and so inexplicable, may have shattered my reason and my nerves, may have withered suddenly within me the joy of prayer—perhaps for ever, who can tell?—may have filled me to the very brim with a dark, more terrible resignation than the worst convulsions of despair in its cataclysmic fall; but my faith is still whole, for I can feel it.[6]

4. Bernanos, *Diary of a Country Priest*, 6.
5. Bernanos, *Diary of a Country Priest*, 28.
6. Bernanos, *Diary of a Country Priest*, 122.

There are times when the priest feels the absence of God. Ironically, God's absence is also a sign of his presence, like waiting for an absent friend but knowing he is somewhere.

Reflecting on the confessions he has heard for six months, he writes that his parishioners merely skim through the surface of their conscience and conceal the "petrification," their hardness of the heart.[7] Expressing his disappointment, he experiences sadness as though his soul were "bleeding to death."[8] He imagines the villagers have "nailed me up here on a cross and are at least watching me die."[9] Feeling helpless, with a deep sense of inadequacy and inferiority, the priest confesses that he is incapable of running a parish. The spiritual malaise of his flock is symbolized by the stomach cancer that eventually kills him.

Due to this disease, the priest can only digest a little bread and wine, which suggests the importance of the Eucharist in sustaining and nourishing the parishioners in the spiritual aridness of the Ambricourt community. The priest works hard in preparing the children for their first communion. He is concerned for the spiritual well-being of the young and the old, sharing their sufferings and conveying the message of God's love and mercy to them. Accepting his weakness, he eventually submits himself to God's merciful love.

The parishioners' lack of faith is the priest's primary concern. Even his sacristan admits that although he and his family are churchgoers, he thinks there is no afterlife. Shocked, the priest writes that the sacristan's words "froze me, and suddenly I had lost heart. I said I felt ill and left him."[10] Despite all these disappointments, the priest does his best to shepherd his flock while blaming himself for his "inexplicable incompetence" and "superhuman clumsiness."[11]

7. Bernanos, *Diary of a Country Priest*, 87.

8. Bernanos, *Diary of a Country Priest*, 87.

9. Bernanos, *Diary of a Country Priest*, 40.

10. Bernanos, *Diary of a Country Priest*, 198.

11. Bernanos, *Diary of a Country Priest*, 190.

Notwithstanding his parishioners' apparent indifference, the priest, a deeply caring and sympathetic individual, prays fervently, longing for God to grant him the ability to truly see and hear the needs of his flock. He writes, "If only the good God would open my eyes and unseal my ears, so that I might behold the face of my parish and hear its voice."[12] The priest's selflessness is evident as he prioritizes the welfare of his parish over his own. Through his prayers, he empathizes with those who are suffering, fostering a deeper communion with God. In his diary, he reflects: "My inner quiet—blessed by God—has never really isolated me. I can feel all humankind can enter."[13]

## Battle of Good and Evil

The priest learns to respond to every "profound spiritual hurt," including that of the unbeliever Dr. Maxence Delbende, with compassion and empathy.[14] This selfless Christian concern takes a toll on him and increases his suffering and pain, especially when Chantal, the daughter of the count and countess, who is filled with anger and hatred, comes to him seeking advice. Aware that she is a "wounded creature," he empathizes with her bitterness, allowing himself to feel her pain, "to let it flood my soul, my heart."[15] In his diary, he says that since the fall into sin, human beings cannot be enlightened "except in the form of agony."[16] Suffering, then, becomes the path through which one can truly empathize with others. The priest knows this cruel young lady, Chantal, is slandering him. Instead of protecting himself, he continues to care for her spiritually, seeing it as a struggle between good and evil.

The priest's spiritual life is also a battleground in the conflict between good and evil: "the world of sin confronts the world of

12. Bernanos, *Diary of a Country Priest*, 28.
13. Bernanos, *Diary of a Country Priest*, 260.
14. Bernanos, *Diary of a Country Priest*, 82.
15. Bernanos, *Diary of a Country Priest*, 133, 134.
16. Bernanos, *Diary of a Country Priest*, 199.

grace. . . . There is not only a communion of saints; there is also a communion of sinners."[17] In his parish, "good and evil are probably evenly distributed."[18] He asserts that though the parish is not dead, it is consumed by boredom, and there is nothing anyone can do about it. Eventually, he becomes aware of "the cancerous growth within us."[19] In his desolation, he seeks counsel from a senior colleague, the curé of Torcy.

## The Curé of Torcy

The young priest regards Torcy as rather worldly, but when the older cleric takes him into a "bare little room" where he prays, the young priest considers him a friend who "could never humiliate a soul."[20] Torcy is a compassionate pastor who cares for the poor and fights for social justice. For his battle against injustice, Torcy was accused of being a "socialist" and driven out of his parish by "pious peasants."[21] However, he is not discouraged and does not care about his disgrace. Seeing his eyes full of tears, the young priest realizes how deep the wound must have been and suffers with Torcy. Admiring Torcy for his love of the poor, the young priest asserts that he "could have kissed his hands" at that very moment. In turn, the older priest tells his protege, "I respect you . . . you've got grit."[22] Although the young priest feels unworthy, he would not betray the trust of his mentor.

Torcy warns the young priest not to believe in progress just because slavery has been abolished, as it will emerge again in another form. He warns that charlatans, who promise to reform the world by word and abolish poverty, are seeking to destroy the weak. Torcy reminds him what Christ said to Judas, "The poor

17. Bernanos, *Diary of a Country Priest*, 138–39.

18. Bernanos, *Diary of a Country Priest*, 1.

19. Bernanos, *Diary of a Country Priest*, 1.

20. Bernanos, *Diary of a Country Priest*, 14, 55.

21. Bernanos, *Diary of a Country Priest*, 57.

22. Bernanos, *Diary of a Country Priest*, 57, 59.

you will always have with you" (Matt 26:11). Judas was "already interested in the pauper problem, like any millionaire."[23] There will always be greedy people like Judas who appear to care for the poor but are really pursuing their own interests.

Concerned for justice, Torcy emanates joy. He sees joy as "the gift of the Church, whatever joy is possible for this sad world to share."[24] However, the suicide of Dr. Delbende, his close friend, causes him great sadness. The young priest notices Torcy's deep sorrow, accompanied by "a truly royal simplicity, . . . an authority, a majesty."[25] His sorrow comes with a "supernatural strength" like the "vast, calm waters under storms."[26] His presence "creates around him a feeling of calm, of peace, of certainty."[27]

Torcy becomes joyful again when he narrates to the young priest the life and character of Dr. Delbende. The doctor, an atheist, is a righteous man who believes that society will never get rid of injustice, and thus, we must fight against it relentlessly. The doctor has paid off an old woman's debt, eleven thousand francs; she was about to lose her land to a businessman.[28] He lost his faith long ago but keeps searching for God among the poor, where the doctor believes he has the best chance of finding him.[29] This act suggests he has not lost faith in God, only in the church.

Olivier, the nephew of the countess and an officer of the Foreign Legion, denounces the church for its complicity in allowing the banks and the state to dominate society. Olivier exposes the hypocrisy of the ruling class for being a "sly effective order, based entirely on cruel knowledge of the resistance of the weak, their capacity for pain, humiliation, and misery."[30] This condemnation of

---

23. Bernanos, *Diary of a Country Priest*, 61.

24. Bernanos, *Diary of a Country Priest*, 20.

25. Bernanos, *Diary of a Country Priest*, 112, 113.

26. Bernanos, *Diary of a Country Priest*, 112, 115.

27. Bernanos, *Diary of a Country Priest*, 112.

28. Bernanos, *Diary of a Country Priest*, 114.

29. Bernanos, *Diary of a Country Priest*, 118.

30. Bernanos, *Diary of a Country Priest*, 244.

the church affects the priest "to the very depths of his heart."[31] Feeling ashamed and weak from vomiting blood, he cries like a child in Olivier's presence. The priest's vulnerability moves the heart of the soldier, who tells him, "You're a good lad. . . . I wouldn't like any priest but you around when I was dying."[32] Olivier then kisses the priest like children do their parents, on both cheeks.

Although a devout Catholic, Bernanos was also critical of the institutional church, which he believed was too preoccupied with status and legalism. This lack of the spirit of Christ is cogently conveyed by Olivier, who believes that the nation has been secularized and is now "the pagan state."[33] He claims that "there is no Christianity . . . because there are no more soldiers. No soldiers, no Christianity. . . . The last real soldier died on May 30, 1431, and you killed her, you people. Not only killed her, condemned her, cut her off, burned her."[34] Olivier is referring to Joan of Arc, whom the priest points out that the church has canonized as a saint. Steadfast in her faith, Joan of Arc, a young girl, demonstrated her strong commitment and holiness, also underscoring the innocence of childhood.

## Spirituality of Torcy

At the heart of Torcy's spirituality is his belief and trust in God. This childlike quality, known as the "Little Way," is found in the life and writing of St. Thérèse of Lisieux (1873–97), a young French Carmelite saint who died of tuberculosis in 1897. It is a fresh interpretation of Jesus's teaching regarding the innocence of a child. Thérèse also teaches us to accept our weakness and suffering with joy and to approach God with the confidence and simplicity of a child. Influenced by Torcy, the young priest adopts this spirituality as he matures.

---

31. Bernanos, *Diary of a Country Priest*, 248.
32. Bernanos, *Diary of a Country Priest*, 248.
33. Bernanos, *Diary of a Country Priest*, 246.
34. Bernanos, *Diary of a Country Priest*, 245.

Devotion to the Blessed Virgin Mary is another characteristic of Torcy's spirituality. The Mother of God, for Torcy, is a model of faith for all believers, especially priests. Torcy's Marian spirituality helps the priest to understand the Virgin's sorrow and acceptance of God's will. Torcy speaks of Mary as having the virtues of innocence and simplicity: "The Virgin was Innocence. . . . The eyes of Our Lady are the only real child eyes that have ever been raised to our shame and sorrow."[35] Torcy refers to her as both our youngest sister and mother as well.

The wisdom and experience of the curé of Torcy complements the priest's naivety: "He [Torcy] is the virile counterpart to the young Curé's diffident sensitivity. . . . In their conversations, it is as if one part of Bernanos were coming to the rescue of the other."[36] In fact, Torcy, an older and wiser pastor, helps the young priest to understand his vocation and spiritual destiny. When Torcy asks his protégé to reflect on his vocation to the priesthood, the priest realizes that he was called to suffer with Christ in his agony at Gethsemane. Overwhelmed, he asks, "Who would dare take such an honour upon himself?"[37]

The differences between Torcy and the young priest demonstrate a shift in Catholic spirituality from a legalistic religion to a more open faith that reaches out to the people.[38] As mentor and friend, Torcy guides his younger colleague towards the spiritual perfection to which they have been called as priests. Thus, inspired by Torcy, the young priest accepts the confidences of those who have fallen, such as the Countess, who resents God for taking away her son and forsaking her to a loveless marriage.

35. Bernanos, *Diary of a Country Priest*, 211.
36. Quoted in Leah, "'Become as a Little Child,'" 253.
37. Bernanos, *Diary of a Country Priest*, 203.
38. Dorschell, "Mentors and Protégés," 5.

## Conversation with the Countess

The dialogue between the priest and the countess on the eve of her death holds great significance as the protagonist fights for the woman's soul. As a sinner, he doubts his worthiness as if "the enemy scorned to hide himself from such a puny adversary, as though he came to defy me openly, laugh in my face."[39] As we shall see, the woman is won over by his tears.

Experiencing intense suffering and anger over the death of her infant son, the countess perceives this tragedy as a great injustice and questions the existence of God. A self-righteous and proud woman, she simply cannot accept her misfortune. Hardened and defiant, she uses her grief as a shield against anyone approaching her. Isolated and indulging in self-pity, she clings tightly to her affliction.

Recognizing his weakness, the priest confronts and challenges the countess. He is concerned that the countess's pride and refusal to accept her son's death may lead to self-destruction. He did not intend to talk about her, but about her daughter, Chantal. He says, "I certainly fear she may be driven to extremes." The countess assures the priest that her daughter will not do such a thing as she fears death, but the priest is not sure and replies that "those are the very ones that kill themselves. . . . Death is a very narrow difficult passage certainly not constructed for the proud." Though afraid to die, he tells the countess, "I fear my own death less than yours."[40]

Accusing the countess of lacking in love, the priest says God will break her hardheartedness. Interestingly, when he softens and becomes emotional, she relents and consoles him. Gaining confidence, the priest is able to direct her spiritually, even though the countess vents her anger against God. Turning her loathing expression into loving assurance, the priest says:

> Madame, . . . if our God were a pagan god or the god of intellectuals—and for me it comes to much the same— He might fly to His remotest heaven and our grief would

39. Bernanos, *Diary of a Country Priest*, 153.
40. Bernanos, *Diary of a Country Priest*, 157.

force Him down to earth again. But you know that our God came to be among us. Shake your fist at Him, spit in His face, scourge Him, and finally crucify Him: what does it matter? *My daughter, it's already been done to Him.*[41]

Further, the priest tells her, "Hell is not to love anymore. As long as we remain in this life, we can still deceive ourselves, think that we love by our own will, that we love independently of God. But we're like madmen stretching out hands to clasp the moon reflected in water."[42]

## Miracle of Our Empty Hands

Recollecting the innocence of childhood, cleansing the bitterness of the past, and purifying one's memory are instrumental to the countess's recovery and return to God. She experiences solace. In their passionate exchange, both the priest and the countess discern their "true childlike natures."[43] The priest's despondency ends when he wins over the countess's soul on her deathbed with a "single tear": "Suddenly I could feel a tear on my cheek, a single tear, as we see them on the faces of the dying, at the furthest limit of their griefs. She watched this tear fall."[44] It reminds us of Christ shedding tears over Jerusalem.

Experiencing peace after talking to the priest, the countess writes a letter to him the following day, sharing her joy in finding a child in him. The countess had lapsed from her Catholic faith and was filled with anger and hatred, but in the end, she cries out in joy, "I've wilfully sinned against hope, every day for eleven years. Yet now I hope again!"[45] She is moved when she sees a tear falling from

41. Bernanos, *Diary of a Country Priest*, 171.

42. Bernanos, *Diary of a Country Priest*, 171.

43. Leah, "'Become as a Little Child,'" 255.

44. Bernanos, *Diary of a Country Priest*, 164.

45. Bernanos, *Diary of a Country Priest*, 175.

the priest's cheek. She writes that she felt spiritually dead after losing a son, but now

> I have lived in the most terrible solitude, alone with the desperate memory of a child. And it seems to me that another child has brought me to life again. I hope you won't be annoyed with me for regarding you as a child. Because you are! May God keep you one for ever![46]

The priest can empathize with the countess's sufferings. This suffering young man is like a child in his weakness. His vulnerability draws out the maternal instinct in the countess, and she responds to him as if he is her son. Her love for her infant son becomes open and reaches out to the other. The priest has never asked her to give up that love but, rather, to reclaim it. When the countess throws the medallion into the fire, the priest rushes to retrieve it, thus hurting himself. He exclaims, "What madness . . . . Do you take God for an executioner? God wants us to be merciful with ourselves. And besides, our sorrows are not our own. He takes them on Himself, into His heart."[47]

The priest's sincere love touches the countess's heart: "the mortal weakness of his life is what is powerful. He is a young man stripped down to his sheer humanity. That is what he offers her. And grace becomes present to her."[48] The peace that the priest bestows as he blesses her is a free gift of God:

> Oh, miracle—thus to be able to give what we ourselves do not possess, sweet miracle of our empty hands! Hope which was shrivelling in my heart flowered again in hers; the spirit of prayer which I thought lost in me for ever, was given back to her by God and—who can tell—perhaps in my name![49]

The countess is able to love again, and her love for her child now extends to the priest. Influenced by the writings of St. Thérèse

46. Bernanos, *Diary of a Country Priest*, 175.

47. Bernanos, *Diary of a Country Priest*, 173.

48. Keegan, "Robert Bresson's *The Diary of a Country Priest*," 54.

49. Bernanos, *Diary of a Country Priest*, 180.

of Lisieux, Bernanos is conveying to his readers the importance of childhood, to "become like children again" (Matt 18:3), and enter the kingdom of heaven.

## Become Like Children Again

On a motorcycle ride with his newfound friend Olivier, the priest delights in excitement, a danger he would have avoided earlier. He feels young again, when "human transcendence dominates one's life."[50] He says, "I realized that youth is blessed—that is a risk worth running, a risk that is also blessed."[51]

In his diary, the priest writes, "I knew that God did not wish me to die without knowing something of that risk—just enough, maybe, for my sacrifice to be complete when the time came."[52] His comprehension of both himself and life as a whole continues to expand, as evidenced in his final diary entry, which reads:

> The strange mistrust I had of myself and of my own be-
> ing, has flown, I believe for ever. That conflict is done. I
> cannot understand it anymore. I am reconciled to my-
> self, to the poor, poor shell of me.
> How easy it is to hate oneself! True grace is to forget.
> Yet if pride could die in us, the supreme grace would be
> to love oneself in all simplicity—as one would love any
> one of those who themselves have suffered and loved in
> Christ.[53]

Embracing his physical awkwardness and personal short-comings, the priest learns to love himself not out of narcissism but as a genuine lover. This transformation becomes evident during the joyful motorcycle ride with Olivier, where the priest rediscovers his forgotten youthfulness amidst his problems and pains. Overwhelmed with the experience, the priest exclaims, "I think

50. Keegan, "Robert Bresson's *The Diary of a Country Priest*," 49.
51. Bernanos, *Diary of a Country Priest*, 235.
52. Bernanos, *Diary of a Country Priest*, 235–36.
53. Bernanos, *Diary of a Country Priest*, 296.

this is what they call joy. Anyway, I felt young, really young, with this companion who was as young as I. We were young together."[54]

The motorcycle ride unveils the beauty and joy of living, allowing him to experience the essence of youthfulness and being:

> I climbed somewhat clumsily onto a small rather uncomfortable seat, and the next minute the long slope we were facing flashed behind us, whilst the roar of the engine rose continuously higher and higher till it gave out one note only, wonderfully pure. It was like the song of light, it was light itself, and I felt I was watching, with my own eyes, the huge curve of that stupendous ascent. The countryside did not come towards us, it opened out on all sides, and just beyond the wild skid of the road, seemed to turn majestically on itself, like a door opening on to another world.[55]

At the beginning of the novel, the priest was a purist in his quest for God. Isolated, he was desperate for spiritual consolation and almost lost hope in achieving it. Karl Rahner describes these people as having

> the secret passion that lives in the real man of the spirit and the saints. They want to savour the experience. In their secret fear of becoming bogged down in the world, they always want to ensure that they are beginning to live in the spirit. They have got the taste of the spirit. . . . The spirit is, as it were, drunk by them pure.

Impatient with mundane life, it is "not as if they too did not always have to return to the ordinariness of everyday living."[56]

The desire for holiness and communion with the Absolute means that we need to return to the world. Gregory Baum stresses this principle: "Man is open to the supernatural not only in an option by which he transcends the finite but in the many necessary

---

54. Bernanos, *Diary of a Country Priest*, 236.

55. Bernanos, *Diary of a Country Priest*, 237.

56. Rahner, *Theological Investigations*, 88.

and often painful choices by which he perseveres in the movement toward growth and reconciliation."[57]

## Grace and Experience

Before grace can be recognized, the priest has to undergo the experience of suffering and purification. Leonardo Boff speaks of experience as "knowledge that has a taste and flavour all its own because it was earned the hard way."[58] Further, he states that,

> It should be evident that experience is not restricted to the senses. It embraces all of life with its dangers and escapes, its challenges and its perplexities. It is not surprising that narration is the best way of communicating the fullness of experience.[59]

Experience is thus a kind of knowledge and awareness; it arises from the encounter between the world and our consciousness.

Grace "emerges within the world in which we ourselves are immersed."[60] It is the reality of God's love and presence in the world. Appearing within our human existence, grace frees us from sin and leads us to life's fullness. Thus, when a person, like the priest, is in a state of grace, his character remains untainted by sin, allowing him to be his authentic self.

## Everything Is Grace

Before his final diary entry, the priest engaged in the recitation of the rosary, invoking the spirit of Mary—a figure of grace and unwavering obedience to God's will—as she uttered the words, "let it be with me according to your word" (Luke 1:38). Despite his seemingly failure-riddled life, the priest's existence can be perceived through the lens of grace, akin to the fulfillment found in

57. Baum, *Man Becoming*, 40.
58. Boff, *Liberating Grace*, 39.
59. Boff, *Liberating Grace*, 40.
60. Boff, *Liberating Grace*, 40.

Mary, who is described as "full of grace" (Luke 1:28). Through the life of this unnamed priest we arrive at a deeper understanding, that genuine love for oneself and God can be attained by embracing the transformative power of loving others.

Before his death, the priest meets an unnamed woman who loves and cares for the ex-priest, Dufréty, who is dying of tuberculosis. In the eyes of the priest, this poor woman is a reflection of the Virgin Mary, even though she says, "I ain't got much religion."[61] Her devotion to Dufréty testifies to her love in the spirit of the gospel. She too is ill and dying, yet she finds joy in serving others. According to Dufréty, the priest used to be rather narrow-minded as a seminarian.[62] But now he tells Dufréty, "If ever I had the misfortune to go back on the vows of my ordination, I would rather it were for the love of a woman than as a result of what you call 'intellectual evolution.'"[63] His acceptance of his friend who has left the priesthood for the love of a woman shows his "openness of youth."[64]

The priest weeps when the doctor informs him that he is dying of stomach cancer. These tears, he realizes, are "tears of love," for he is leaving for a place filled with "rivers of light and shadow bearing the dreams of the poor."[65] Accepting himself as he is, he understands that his weaknesses are, in fact, his virtues: "I have always known that I possessed the spirit of poverty. The spirit of childhood is much akin. No doubt they are really one and the same thing."[66] In this novel, George Bernanos teaches us that the priesthood is actually about the power of self-sacrifice and dying for others.

The priest jots down thoughts of childhood memories in his diary and the need to recapture that spirit. Gaining confidence, he

---

61. Bernanos, *Diary of a Country Priest*, 287.

62. Bernanos, *Diary of a Country Priest*, 277.

63. Bernanos, *Diary of a Country Priest*, 283–84.

64. Keegan, "Robert Bresson's *The Diary of a Country Priest*," 49.

65. Bernanos, *Diary of a Country Priest*, 276, 275.

66. Bernanos, *Diary of a Country Priest*, 280.

experiences joy and accepts the past with no regrets, "small joys that release me."[67] He expresses his thoughts on death:

> I do not turn my back on death, neither do I confront it bravely as M. Olivier surely would. I have tried to open my eyes to death in all the simplicity of surrender, yet with no secret wish to soften or disarm it. Were the comparison less foolish, I would say that I look upon death as I did on Sulpice Mitonnet or Mile Chantal. . . . Alas, one would need also to become as a little child.[68]

When death approaches, he requests his friend Dufréty administer the last rite. Dufréty is no longer in the priesthood and is living with a woman. Before his conversion, the priest would have been shocked at the idea because it contradicted the church's teaching. Now the end is near, he is at peace with himself, "Does it matter? Grace is . . . everywhere."[69]

No longer loathing himself, he has accepted himself as he is: "How easy it is to hate oneself! True grace is to forget. Yet if pride could die in us, the supreme grace would be to love oneself in all simplicity—as one would love any one of those who themselves have suffered and loved in Christ."[70] In experiencing the grace of God, the priest once again recovers the simplicity and innocence of a child. Surrendering himself, he has accepted death calmly.

67. Bernanos, *Diary of a Country Priest*, 293.
68. Bernanos, *Diary of a Country Priest*, 293.
69. Bernanos, *Diary of a Country Priest*, 298.
70. Bernanos, *Diary of a Country Priest*, 296.

Chapter 6

# The "Whisky Priest" in *The Power and the Glory*

GRAHAM GREENE (1904–91), REGARDED by many as one of the leading English novelists of the twentieth century, was born in Berkhamsted, Hertfordshire, England and died in Vevey, Switzerland. Greene attended Berkhamsted School, where his father was the headmaster. After studying at Balliol College, Oxford, he was converted to Roman Catholicism under the influence of Vivien Dayrell-Browning, whom he married in 1927. He worked as a copyeditor for *The Times* in London from 1926 to 1930. Greene's first novel was *The Man Within* (1929), later adapted as the movie *The Smugglers* (1947). Leaving *The Times*, he worked as a film critic and editor for *The Spectators* till 1940. For the next three decades, he was a freelance journalist and writer, frequently travelling abroad.[1]

As the son of the headmaster, Graham was often bullied at school, and because of this trauma, his writing is characterized by fear and anxiety: "And so faith came to one—shapelessly, without dogma, a presence above a croquet lawn; something associated

---

1. *Encyclopedia Britannica Online*, s.v. "Graham Greene," https://www.britannica.com/biography/Graham-Greene. The material in this chapter appeared in Mong, *Christianity and Western Literature*, 133–51.

with violence, cruelty, evil across the way. One began to believe in heaven because one believed in hell, but for a long while, it was only hell one could picture with a certain intimacy, . . . one began slowly, painfully, reluctantly to populate heaven."[2] Harassed and depressed, Greene developed a suicidal tendency. His picture of hell is drawn from this harrowing existence, enhanced by literary inspiration.

Greene regarded himself as a Catholic who happened to write novels and not a Catholic writer as such. However, "if Catholicism is not the very fabric of many of his texts, it is always a thread that helps to bind literary preoccupations into a recognizable pattern."[3] Many of the characters in his novels are isolated Catholics who ponder damnation and redemption. Greene claimed that religious belief gives greater intensity and force to his characters than non-believers.[4] Consequently in his writings, he created his personal religious system in juxtaposition with the tenets of Catholicism.[5]

Thus, some critics accused Greene of heresies, such as Jansenism or Manicheanism, because "the space between the fallen nature of Greene's characters and the mysterious, inscrutable grace of God was too wide a theological gap to be countenanced, and Greene's disdain for traditional expressions of Catholic faith and piety portrayed throughout his novels proved troubling to many in the pre-Vatican II discourse of the Catholic Church."[6] Detractors doubted the authenticity of Greene's Catholicism, given how he challenged Catholic orthodoxy. Be that as it may, fiction can sometimes surpass official church teaching in conveying the reality of sin, forgiveness, and redemption, and Greene's novels are exemplars.

The novels of Greene that are strongly influenced by his Catholic background include *Brighton Rock* (1938), *The Power and*

2. Quoted in Bergonzi, *Study in Greene*, 105.

3. Bosco, "From *The Power and the Glory* to *The Honorary Consul*," 51.

4. Bergonzi, *Study in Greene*, 117.

5. Baldridge, *Graham Greene's Fictions*, 4.

6. Bosco, "From *The Power and the Glory* to *The Honorary Consul*," 52.

*the Glory* (1940), *The Heart of the Matter* (1948), and *The End of the Affair* (1951). In these writings, Greene displays a consistent concern with sin and moral failure played out in squalid places that are dangerous and violent. The moral and spiritual struggles of his protagonists are set within a volatile political context that enhances the conflict within the individuals. Inhabiting a fallen world, Greene's characters experience the presence of evil as an intense force. "His deepest concerns were spiritual: a soul working out its salvation or damnation amid the paradoxes and anomalies of twentieth-century existence."[7]

A superb storyteller, Greene wrote thrillers featuring crimes and conspiracy, with thought-provoking dialogues incorporated within a fast-paced narrative. He greatly influenced many authors around the world, one of whom is Japanese writer Shusaku Endo. Known for his 1966 historical novel *Silence*, which was adapted into a film in 2016 by the director Martin Scorsese, Shusaku Endo is known as "the Japanese Graham Greene."[8] Like *The Power and the Glory*, *Silence* also features a fugitive priest undergoing spiritual and moral struggles in the midst of fierce religious persecution, which is politically motivated. The Jesuit in *Silence*, too, falters in his priestly vocation as he confronts the terrifying prospect of martyrdom.

Focusing on *The Power and the Glory*, this chapter examines the difficulty of faith in the midst of persecution and poverty, the issues of sin and salvation, and the nature of priesthood as characterized in the figure of the "bad" priest. Yet, in spite of the ruthless suppression of the church and the priest's moral failure, his execution paradoxically represents the triumph of Christianity. Literary critic Terry Eagleton asserts that failure is "one legitimate form of victory" in Greene's novels.[9] Thus, the priest seems to have "a vested interest in failure," as we shall see in the following discussion.[10] Reading like a detective story set in southern Mexico, with

7. "Graham Greene, 86, Dies," para. 9.
8. Link, "Bad Priests and the Valor of Pity," 75.
9. Bosco, "From *The Power and the Glory* to *The Honorary Consul*," 57.
10. Finn, "Graham Greene as Moralist, 23.

the police pursuing the priest, *The Power and the Glory* is full of surprises and suspense.

## Mexico

Graham Greene went to Mexico in the spring of 1930 to write a book on the condition of the Catholic Church in that country, where for several years it was persecuted by an anti-religious government. Travelling in remote regions and experiencing physical hardship, he wrote his masterpiece, *The Power and the Glory*. This novel, a powerful story based on his observations during a five-month trip to Tabasco in 1938, is "vivid, conveying physical sensations with painful immediacy."[11] In spite of the harsh conditions and the suffering he witnessed, Greene's visit to Mexico deepened his Catholic faith.

For Greene, there is a difference between faith and belief: "faith . . . means an unquestioning acceptance of God and a trust in His love and mercy. Belief, on the other hand, is man's rationalisation and institutionalisation of God through theology and the Church."[12] Faith, a gift from God, is a spontaneous and instinctive response to the divine, while belief involves dogma and formula. "Faith, one was told, could move mountains, and here was faith—faith in the spittle that healed the blind man and the voice that raised the dead."[13] In the novel, belief associated with rituals seems mechanical and ceases to be vital to faith. Greene also maintained that he was "inclined to find superstition or magic more 'rational' than such abstract religious ideas as the Holy Trinity." He preferred the "primitive manifestations of the faith."[14] *The Power and the Glory* reveals his preference for the vivid and violent manifestation of faith.

---

11. Bergonzi, *Study in Greene*, 103.
12. Quoted in Baldridge, *Graham Greene's Fictions*, 59.
13. Greene, *Power and the Glory*, 155.
14. Quoted in Baldridge, *Graham Greene's Fictions*, 59.

In the 1930s, the revolutionary government in Mexico was hell-bent on destroying Catholicism and declaring socialism and atheism as the guiding principles for the nation. This new policy meant that priests had to apostatize or face death. In the story, the government appears to be successful in its campaign to eradicate religion as we witness empty church buildings with no priests in sight. The only priest we encounter is the "whisky priest," a morally weak cleric who has given in to the temptation of the flesh and is incompetent in performing his pastoral duties. Yet, he chooses to remain in the socialist state, which is embodied in the person of the police lieutenant who pursues him relentlessly. The priest succeeds in evading the police for some time, even when he is thrown in prison for a minor offence and is released subsequently. He also succeeds in crossing over to a more tolerant state but is compelled to return to hear the confession of a criminal, knowing full well that he will be arrested and executed eventually.

As the whisky priest faces death by the firing squad, he looks back at his life with painful disappointment. Unable to confess his sins to another priest, Padre Jose, who is too terrified to attend to him, the priest thinks he will end up in hell. But Greene seems to say that our salvation does not depend on formula or ritual but on the mercy of God. Contrasting the figure of a guilt-ridden priest with allegorical or flat characters, Greene is able to present the story of sin and salvation, and corruption and contrition, in a dramatic and hypnotic way. While the priest is trying to evade being captured by the police, we can feel that the power of grace is also simultaneously pursuing him.

## Archetypal Characters

The journey of the priest can be perceived allegorically as the way of the cross, or in terms of Dantean circles, moving from hell and purgatory to paradise. Whichever way we take it, the fundamental approach to measure the priest's torturous path is "to recognize that he carries his spiritual fidelity like a temptation among various contrasting characters."[15] In other words, during the priest's pilgrimage, he meets different persons who reveal to him (and the reader) the various aspects of his character and the distance he has travelled towards his destination.

The priest first meets the dentist, Mr. Tench, who feels forsaken and desires to escape from his oppressive environment. His name, Tench, sounds like a stench, which he has to endure as a dentist. In a land festering with buzzards, Tench makes his living by treating tooth decay. As he spends his life looking into the depths of human decay, he, too, wants to escape. But unlike the priest, he is more interested in saving his pesos than his soul. Both Tench and the priest have observed the boat leaving, but they are obliged to remain in the wretched town for different reasons. For the priest, it is his pastoral duty; for Tench, it is his personal monetary considerations.

Coral Fellows, a thirteen-year-old girl, tells the priest that she lost her faith at age ten. Very mature for her age, she takes good care of her mother and those who need her: "She was ready to accept any responsibility, even that of vengeance, without a second thought. It was her life."[16] It is a significant encounter as Coral provides the priest with food, drink, and refuge and helps him to escape. Even though she has lost her Protestant faith, she is compassionate and sympathetic towards the plight of the priest. Coral said, "I hope you'll escape. . . . If they kill you I shan't forgive them—ever."[17]

The priest returns to the village where he has fathered a child. He has experienced lust for the person of Maria, who gave birth to Brigida, his daughter. Seeing his child for the first time after six years, he feels as if he were "seeing his own mortal sin look back at him, without contrition."[18] The priest is concerned that his child would face corruption when she discovers that "the world was in her heart already, like the small spot of decay in a fruit. She

15. Gaston, *Pursuit of Salvation*, 30.
16. Greene, *Power and the Glory*, 42.
17. Greene, *Power and the Glory*, 42.
18. Greene, *Power and the Glory*, 67.

was without protection—she had no grace, no charm to plead for her; his heart was shaken by the conviction of loss. . . . He prayed silently, 'O God, give me any kind of death—without contrition, in a state of sin—only save this child.'"[19] Through this act of uncondi-tional and sacrificial love, we discover God's true nature: "one must love every soul as if it were one's own child." The priest also feels "tethered and aching" love for his child.[20] Unable to provide his child with a secure home, he trusts God's divine mercy.

Upon meeting the half-caste, who turns out to be Judas, the traitor, instead of reacting with anger and self-pity, the priest real-izes his tendency to such treacherous deeds. He attempts to under-stand and accept his betrayer: "Christ had died for this man too: how could he pretend with his pride and lust and cowardice to be any more worthy of that death than this half-caste?"[21] Looking at his betrayer, the priest experiences a vision of divine love, which helps him to show charity to every sinner he encounters.

The priest's pilgrimage is also a "process of purgation."[22] During one night in a prison cell, he finds himself in the presence of many other offenders, which reveals his past sins and the sins of humanity in general. Nevertheless, these inmates are related to him as fellow sinners who should be accepted and loved. The priest's sympathy is shown when he empathizes with and defends a couple making love in a dark corner of the cell, while a respect-able middle-class woman, who is jailed for possessing religious books in her home, is scandalized: "Because suddenly we discover that our sins have so much beauty" and "Hate was just a failure of imagination."[23]

The prison presents the reality of life to the priest: "this place was very like the world: overcrowded with lust and crime and un-happy love: it stank to heaven; but he realized that after all it was possible to find peace there, when you knew for certain that the

19. Greene, *Power and the Glory*, 82.
20. Greene, *Power and the Glory*, 82.
21. Greene, *Power and the Glory*, 99.
22. Gaston, *Pursuit of Salvation*, 31.
23. Greene, *Power and the Glory*, 130–31.

time was short."[24] The experience in prison has a significant effect
on him as he acquires a profound sense of solidarity with sinners:
"He was just one criminal among a herd of criminals, . . . he had
a sense of companionship which he had never received in the old
days when pious people came kissing his black cotton glove."[25]
Although the people in prison have committed sins of lust, anger,
pride, etc., the priest is able to discover beauty as he tells the pious
lady who is disturbed by the couple having sex:

> Such a lot of beauty. Saints talk about the beauty of suf-
> fering. Well, we are not saints, you and I. Suffering to us
> is just ugly. Stench and crowding and pain. That is beau-
> tiful in that corner—to them. It needs a lot of learning to
> see things with a saint's eye: a saint gets a subtle taste for
> beauty and can look down on poor ignorant palates like
> theirs. But we can't afford to.[26]

Here we witness the priest possessing the feelings of holiness
and humility. His humility moves him to escape the police and flee
to another state. Seeing himself as a sinner, staying put would be
an insult to God and the church that he represents. Crossing the
border, he finds a place of refuge with the Lehr family: "Mr. Lehr
had left Germany when he was a boy to escape military service: he
had a shrewd lined idealistic face. You needed to be shrewd in this
country if you were going to retain any ideals at all: he was cun-
ning in the defence of the good life."[27] But the priest is not satisfied
with this kind of comfortable life and remembers the night in the
crowded cell filled with fellow sinners.

Once the priest enters into the safe territory where the Lehr
family lives, free from physical harm, as he recalls the past, he becomes aware of the spiritual danger that comes with a comfortable
lifestyle: "He felt respect all the way up the street: men took off
their hats as he passed: it was as if he had got back to the days
before the persecution. He could feel the old life hardening round

24. Greene, *Power and the Glory*, 125.
25. Greene, *Power and the Glory*, 128.
26. Greene, *Power and the Glory*, 130.
27. Greene, *Power and the Glory*, 161.

him like a habit, a stony case which held his head high and dictated the way he walked, and even formed his words."[28] Ironically, the priest feels relief when the half-caste appears to lure him back across the border, where he would be arrested.

In his writings, Greene often explores geographical frontiers with peace and safety on one side and danger and death on the other. There are also non-physical boundaries that he examines, such as the difference between Catholicism and Communism, success and failure, faith and doubt, trust and betrayal. In this case, Greene considers the "temptation" that lures the priest back to the dangerous spot. This consideration reveals his "sympathy with the seedy, the outcast, the apparently disloyal, a sympathy that has at times come close to collusion. He seems, indeed, to have a vested interest in failure."[29]

Thus the appearance of the half-caste seems like a temptation he cannot resist: "the temptation of self-sacrifice."[30] The return of the Judas figure is a clear sign that God, not the lieutenant, is the real hunter. Aware that it is a trap, the priest actually "felt quite cheerful: he had never really believed in this peace. He had dreamed of it so often on the other side that now it meant no more to him than a dream. He began to whistle a tune—something he had heard somewhere once. 'I found a rose in my field': it was time he woke up."[31] Thus the priest returns to minister to the needy, convinced that it is God's will.

As a cleric without a name, he represents the vocation of the priesthood, which he fulfills as best as he can despite his defects and moral failings. According to the Letter to the Hebrews, "For we do not have a high priest who is unable to sympathize with our weaknesses, but we have one who in every respect has been tested as we are, yet without sin" (4:5). The only perfect person is Christ, the high priest who understands our frailty. The whisky priest is not the Lord, but a sinful human being struggling to fulfill his

28. Greene, *Power and the Glory*, 167–68.
29. Finn, "Graham Greene as Moralist," 23.
30. Gaston, *Pursuit of Salvation*, 33.
31. Greene, *Power and the Glory*, 180.

vocation while facing difficulties and temptations. The bishop and almost all the other priests have fled to safety. Only he remains. This priest is contrasted with Padre Jose, who, following the government's demands, has abandoned the priesthood and married. Padre Jose is even afraid to hear the confession of the priest waiting to be executed.

The death of this "bad priest" is contrasted with that of Juan, a saintly priest that appears in a pious book that a mother reads to her son. The boy is also the one who welcomes a new priest into the country. This signifies to us that the mission of the church continues. Tertullian, a second-century church father, says, "The blood of the martyrs is the seed of the church." The mission of the church continues in Mexico today due to the examples of martyrdom, the glorious one like that of Juan and the "inglorious death" of the nameless priest.[32] They are all instrumental to the spread of the Christian faith amid fierce persecution by a godless and totalitarian government.

## Martyrdom

"The Mexicans are not only the people who killed the martyrs; they are the people for whom the martyrs died."[33] *The Power and the Glory* is also about the journey of a modern martyr, a nameless Mexican priest, who acknowledges his sinfulness but continues to minister to his people in disguise, celebrating Masses and hearing confessions. He embarks on this mission of mercy, knowing well that he will be arrested and killed. Eventually, like Christ, he is betrayed, interrogated, and executed.

Greene attempts to portray this flawed cleric, who has been denied absolution before he is executed, as a martyr. Drunk and desperate, when taken to his execution, "you could tell that he was doing his best—it was only that his legs were not fully under his

32. Leah, "Bad Priest?" 21.

33. Quoted in Bergonzi, *Study in Greene*, 110.

control."[34] The whisky priest could be considered a martyr because he responds to the call of duty as a priest at the cost of his own life. Greene considers him a saint as well:

> He felt only an immense disappointment because he had to go to God empty-handed, with nothing done at all. It seemed to him at that moment that it would have been quite easy to have been a saint. It would only have needed a little self-restraint and a little courage. He felt like someone who has missed happiness by seconds at an appointed place. He knew now that at the end there was only one thing that counted—to be a saint.[35]

Greene upholds the church's teaching that a man should be distinguished from his office. *The Power and the Glory* examines the nature of the Catholic priesthood and the sacraments. The priest character in the novel is "ontological in nature," set apart not by his virtue but by his sacramental function.[36] When Coral asks the priest to renounce his priesthood to save himself, he replies, "It's impossible. There's no way. I'm a priest. It's out of my power."[37]

*Ex opere operato* is a Latin expression that means "by the work worked." The sacraments confer grace when the sign is validly effected. The sacraments take effect as long as the priest celebrates the Mass, hears confessions, etc., using the proper form and formula. Its validity does not depend on the character of the priest administering it. The priest in the novel admits his unworthiness—he is a "whisky priest," fond of drinking, and has fathered a child. However, instead of fleeing to other states where he would be safe, or abandoning the priesthood to remain alive, he persists in bringing the sacraments to his flock in spite of the danger.

Further, the priest is contrite and humble, and he never fails to mortify himself when his conscience comes into play. He tells the lieutenant he is proud to be the only priest remaining in the province when others have fled. He disagrees when the lieutenant

34. Greene, *Power and the Glory*, 216.
35. Greene, *Power and the Glory*, 210.
36. Bosco, "From *The Power and the Glory* to *The Honorary Consul*," 63.
37. Greene, *Power and the Glory*, 40.

says he will be a martyr: "Oh, no. Martyrs are not like me. They don't think all the time—if I had drunk more brandy I shouldn't be so afraid."[38]

*The Power and the Glory* exposes the "paradoxes of saint-hood" when we witness a fallen priest who goes against the in-stinct of self-preservation and dies for his faith.[39] God makes use of the weak to accomplish his work. St. Paul says, "For the sake of Christ, then, I am content with weaknesses, insults, hardships, persecutions, and calamities; for when I am weak, then I am strong" (2 Cor 12:10). Thus the lieutenant and the half-caste who are responsible for the priest's death are also part of God's purpose. In other words, they are part of the divine providence where God is present in all human actions. Greene writes:

> But at the centre of his own faith there always stood the convincing mystery—that we were made in God's im-age—God was the parent, but He was also the police-man, the criminal, the priest, the maniac, and the judge. Something resembling God dangled from the gibbet or went into odd attitudes before the bullets in a prison yard or contorted itself like a camel in the attitude of sex. He would sit in the confessional and hear the complicated dirty ingenuities which God's image had thought out: and God's image shook now, up and down on the mule's back, with the yellow teeth sticking out over the lower lip; and God's image did its despairing act of rebellion with Maria in the hut among the rats.[40]

Since all human actions are images of God, then the respon-sibility of the character is limited. They all share in this "inescap-able existence conditioned by their Maker."[41] Thus, individuals cannot be judged or distinguished solely by their actions. If we believe in God, *The Power and the Glory* is not just a thriller about

---

38. Greene, *Power and the Glory*, 196.

39. Pryce-Jones, *Graham Greene*, 57.

40. Greene, *Power and the Glory*, 101.

41. Pryce-Jones, *Graham Greene*, 58.

a policeman chasing after a priest in Mexico but a divine comedy addressing our fall and redemption.

Infused with Christian imagery, the main characters do not have names—they are allegorical figures. Contrasting the idealism of the lieutenant to the fatalism of the priest, both characters stand by their beliefs to the end. The lieutenant sincerely believes that he kills to protect the people while the whisky priest continues to give life in his mission. The allegory emerges to reinforce the Christian story: the priest who has been betrayed, suffered, and died for his sins, has saved and converted others by his good example. The lieutenant, like Pilate, falls asleep due to exhaustion: "He couldn't remember afterwards anything of his dreams except laughter."[42] The American criminal, Calver, sounds like Calvary, and the two photographs at the police station remind us of Christ and Barabbas.

## Dostoevskian Echoes

In *The Power and the Glory*, which appears to show the triumph of Christianity over secularism, we hear echoes of the Russian novelist Fyodor Dostoevsky resounding in some of Greene's characters. For example, the discussion between the priest and the police lieutenant regarding ultimate values in Greene's novel reminds us of the conversation between Christ and the Grand Inquisitor in *The Brothers Karamazov*. The incompatibility of their beliefs is well depicted in this exchange:

> "We've always said the poor are blessed and the rich are going to find it hard to get into heaven. Why should we make it hard for the poor man too? Oh, I know we are told to give to the poor, to see they are not hungry—hunger can make a man do evil just as much as money can. But why should we give the poor power? It's better to let him die in dirt and wake in heaven—so long as we don't push his face in the dirt."

42. Greene, *Power and the Glory*, 207.

"I hate your reasons," the lieutenant said. "I don't want reasons. If you see somebody in pain, people like you reason and reason. You say—perhaps pain's a good thing, perhaps he'll be better for it one day. I want to let my heart speak."

"At the end of a gun."

"Yes. At the end of a gun."

"Oh, well, perhaps when you're my age you'll know the heart's an untrustworthy beast. The mind is too, but it doesn't talk about love. Love. And a girl puts her head under water or a child's strangled, and the heart all the time says love, love."[43]

Like the priest's secular counterpart, the lieutenant "was a mystic, too, and what he had experienced was vacancy—a complete certainty in the existence of a dying, cooling world, of human beings who had evolved from animals for no purpose at all."[44]

As in Dostoevsky's novel, Greene uses "mirroring and doubling" as a structural device.[45] The priest and the lieutenant both stand in opposition to each other by their beliefs as well as their social and political circumstances. It is the duty and responsibility of the lieutenant to arrest whomever he believes to be the last active priest in the region. He says, "We do more good when we catch one of these [priests]" than catching the American bank robber and murderer.[46] Unlike the hedonistic priest, the lieutenant is an ascetic: "he felt no need of women" and the room where he lives is "as comfortless as a prison or a monastic cell."[47] In fact, he "felt no sympathy at all with the weakness of the flesh."[48]

The lieutenant still remembers "the smell of incense in the churches of his boyhood, the candles and the laciness and the self-esteem, the immense demands made from the altar steps by

43. Greene, *Power and the Glory*, 199.

44. Greene, *Power and the Glory*, 24–25.

45. Pellow, "'Presence' of Dostoevsky," 59.

46. Greene, *Power and the Glory*, 23.

47. Greene, *Power and the Glory*, 23–24.

48. Greene, *Power and the Glory*, 25.

men who didn't know the meaning of sacrifice."[49] Regarding his attitude towards religious belief, which is practical and rational, the lieutenant resembles the Grand Inquisitor.

The priest is concerned with saving the souls of his flock, even though he endangers some in the process. On the other hand, the lieutenant is determined to improve his people's lives, especially those of the children: "It infuriated him to think that there were still people in the state who believed in a loving and merciful God."[50] He believes the children "deserved nothing less than the truth—a vacant universe and a cooling world, the right to be happy in any way they chose."[51] His method is similar to the Grand Inquisitor in that he would provide "bread" for the people and secure their obedience by means of fear, not freedom.

With good intentions, the lieutenant is determined to eradicate what he perceives as the evil of the church and her teaching: "No more money for saying prayers, no more money for building places to say prayers in. We'll give people food instead, teach them to read, give them books. We'll see they don't suffer."[52] But the priest believes suffering is part and parcel of life, whether in the secular or sacred sphere:

> It's no good your working for your end unless you're a good man yourself. And there won't always be good men in your party. Then you'll have all the old starvation, beating, get-rich-anyhow. But it doesn't matter so much my being a coward—and all the rest. I can put God into a man's mouth just the same—and I can give him God's pardon. It wouldn't make any difference to that if every priest in the Church was like me.[53]

Here again, Greene distinguishes the man and the sacrament he administers, putting "God into man's mouth," and giving him

49. Greene, *Power and the Glory*, 22.
50. Greene, *Power and the Glory*, 24.
51. Greene, *Power and the Glory*, 58.
52. Greene, *Power and the Glory*, 94.
53. Greene, *Power and the Glory*, 195.

"God's pardon." It does not matter if the priest is bad, the sacraments he confers are valid all the same.

The lieutenant admires the priest's conviction and fidelity but sees no meaning in it. Like the priest, he has dedicated his life to justice. As they journey back to the city for trial and execution, the lieutenant tells the priest that even his God is not grateful for his service and has rewarded his loyalty with cruelty. Then accepting his fate and believing in the mystery of God's grace, the priest says, "I don't know a thing about the mercy of God: I don't know how awful the human heart looks to Him. But I do know this—that if there's ever been a single man in this state damned, then I'll be damned too. . . . I wouldn't want it to be any different. I just want justice, that's all."[54] Despite human failure and uncontrolled passion, the priest "knew now that at the end there was only one thing that counted—to be a saint."[55]

As a channel of grace, the priest's presence has a benign influence on those around him, a spiritual power that energizes souls. He brings "back to . . . secular and desiccated consciousness an impression of spiritual greatness and possibility, indirectly moving them, perhaps at an unconscious level, to a greater spiritual moment in themselves."[56] For example, after a chance encounter with the priest, Mr. Tench, the dentist, decides to contact his wife, whom he has not seen for years: "an odd impulse had come to him to project this stray letter towards the last address he had. . . . He tried to begin. . . . He began to write . . . ."[57] Coral Fellows, who harbours the outlaw priest, is given an opportunity to discuss religion. This moves her to reflect on her abandoned faith.[58]

54. Greene, *Power and the Glory*, 200.

55. Greene, *Power and the Glory*, 210.

56. Quoted in Baldridge, *Graham Greene's Fictions*, 61.

57. Greene, *Power and the Glory*, 45–46.

58. Greene, *Power and the Glory*, 41.

## Paradox

In the novel, the priest serves as the embodiment of belief, and the police lieutenant of unbelief. A paradoxical figure, the priest possesses a "double rhythm of hope and despair, action and passivity, vaunting ambition and victimization, longing for escape and for capture, obsession equally with the diurnal and the transcendent moment."[59] A morally weak individual who is addicted to alcohol and has fathered a child, the priest is mediocre at best.

On the other hand, the lieutenant, the priest's counterpart, is a puritanical law enforcer who has dedicated his life to his socialist ideals. Being a celibate and performing his police duties with religious zeal, he would have been an ideal candidate for the priesthood: "There was something of a priest in his intent observant walk—a theologian going back over the errors of the past to destroy them again."[60] Indeed, Greene stresses the lieutenant's asceticism, dedication, and honesty.

The lieutenant's anti-clericalism stems from his conviction that the church is solely responsible for the injustice in the country. He perceives the priesthood as a corrupt system that benefits only a few. To arrest a priest, the lieutenant would go to the extent of shooting hostages. At the same time, he offers to bring Padre Jose to hear the confession of the whisky priest before his execution.

Like the French existentialists, such as Albert Camus and Jean-Paul Sartre, Greene struggles with a world that seems meaningless—a dystopia, as it were. However, his Catholic faith gives him hope and, in some ways, offsets "the vacancy and aridity he so powerfully describes."[61] Without this faith and doubt, his writings would lack passion and purpose. Yet, aware of the difficulties of faith, Greene also experiences the desperation of disbelief. Greene thinks that the human "predicament is paradoxical."[62] In other

---

59. Quoted in Cloete, "Religious Paradoxes," 318.
60. Greene, *Power and the Glory*, 24.
61. Quoted in St. Amant, "God Gets His Man," 56.
62. St. Amant, "God Gets His Man," 57.

words, a person's goodness and greatness are intermingled with their greatness and wretchedness.

An Augustinian, Greene seems to hold that the fall of humanity is not just the loss of faith, hope, and charity but a corruption that leads to lust and pride. At the same time, the human person, too, feels a sense of responsibility and shame and seeks to save him- or herself. Pascal maintains that "Christianity is strange. It bids man recognize that he is vile, even abominable, and bids him desire to be like God. Without such a counterpoise, this dignity would make him horribly vain, or this humiliation would make him terribly abject."[63] This paradox is portrayed in *The Power and the Glory* when the priest reflects on the anomaly of his clerical state. "Looked at rationally, the priest is all too often a mess—but it is here, in spite of all, that we see the power and the glory in a world of saints and sinners."[64]

For Greene, the person is simultaneously good and evil, an ambiguity that is powerfully played out in his novel. His characters are not mere mechanical entities; they experience the conflict between good and evil and thus have to make their choice. In *The Power and the Glory*, the priest, deeply aware of his sinfulness, attempts to flee from God: "Evil ran like malaria in his veins."[65] However, he tells himself, "In three days . . . I shall have confessed and been absolved."[66] The priest admits that he has more pride than he has love of God.[67] But Paul says, "where sin increased, grace abounded all the more" (Rom 5:21). Thus, in the end, "the bad priest" realizes that to be a saint is what really matters.

63. Quoted in St. Amant, "God Gets His Man," 57–58.
64. Jasper, "Priest in the Novels of Graham Greene," 84.
65. Greene, *Power and the Glory*, 176.
66. Greene, *Power and the Glory*, 176.
67. Greene, *Power and the Glory*, 196.

## The "Bad Priest"

There are good priests and bad priests. It is just that I am
a bad priest.[68]

The figure of the bad priest is not just an archetype but a terrifying reality; we have witnessed the spate of clerical abuses and
misconduct throughout history. He is a character clearly "fraught
with background."[69] In fact, bad priests have always been part of
the fabric of religious life. In the Old Testament, the bad priest
appears almost immediately after the institution of the priesthood.
Apostasy occurred when Aaron, the chief priest, yielded to the demands of the Israelites to build the golden calf (Exod 32). Aaron,
the traditional founder and head of the Israelite priesthood, became the first person to violate the covenant, thus breaking the
command, "You shall not make for yourself an idol, whether in
the form of anything that is in heaven above, or that is on the earth
beneath, or that is in the water under the earth" (Exod 20:4). In the
New Testament, the Pharisees and the Sadducees, the high priests,
Annas and Caiaphas, are examples of bad priests in the biblical
tradition.

In Western literature, such as the writings of Boccaccio and
Chaucer, we find the figure of the bad priest portrayed as a buf-
foon, the "reverent rake."[70] Historical figures like Tomás de Torque-
mada of the Spanish Inquisition and the Grand Inquisitor in *The
Brothers Karamazov* are well known for their zeal in torturing and
burning heretics. Unfortunately, the reality of the bad priest in the
Catholic Church has been constantly in the media in the last few
decades to the extent that the good priest is sometimes perceived
as the exception rather than the norm. This widespread abuse and
misconduct by bad priests has grievously hurt the church's credibility, leading to a crisis of faith among many believers.

68. Greene, *Power and the Glory*, 191.
69. Quoted in Link, "Bad Priests and the Valor of Pity," 79.
70. Link, "Bad Priests and the Valor of Pity," 80.

In *The Power and the Glory*, however, the portrayal of the bad priest is meant to be "a theological test case of the limits of divine mercy."[71] He bears the "emblematic weight of sin, brought . . . fully to consciousness in the commission."[72] The bad priest in Greene's novel is an example of what German theologian Karl Rahner calls "man as a being threatened radically by guilt."[73] The presence of the bad priest serves the purpose of leading the reader to reflect on the question of redemption and damnation.

The portrayal of the bad priest is Greene's attempt to present the Christian paradox (Rom 5:6–10) and theodicy, justifying God in the face of evil. This theodicy is reflected in the sermon given by the priest to a group of peasants:

> Pray that you will suffer more and more and more. Never get tired of suffering. The police watching you, the soldiers gathering taxes, the beating you always get from the jefe because you are too poor to pay, smallpox and fever, hunger, . . . that is all part of heaven—the preparation. Perhaps without them—who can tell?—you wouldn't enjoy heaven so much. Heaven would not be complete.[74]

The priest, believing himself to be bad, cut off from grace, unaware of his virtue, is, in reality, a compassionate person, willing to sacrifice his life for others. He is an example of what Christ teaches: "do not let your left hand know what your right hand is doing" (Matt 6:3).

## The Catholic Novel

Muriel Spark, a Catholic novelist, said there is no such thing as a "Catholic Novel." George Orwell thought Catholics were unlikely to be good writers because their religious tradition or "the atmosphere of orthodoxy" might hinder their creativity. Orwell claimed

71. Link, "Bad Priests and the Valor of Pity," 80.
72. Link, "Bad Priests and the Valor of Pity," 81.
73. Quoted in Link, "Bad Priests and the Valor of Pity," 81.
74. Greene, *Power and the Glory*, 69.

that the novel is, in fact, a Protestant literary form, the product of a free and independent mind.[75] But as we have seen, the tension created by orthodoxy and free thinking can be creative, imaginative, and inspiring in prose writing, as Graham Greene has shown us in his novel.

In its effort to control literary work, the Catholic Church almost banned *The Power and the Glory*. The Vatican was trying to prevent heresy, which had spread into the academic world. The Holy Office considered the book dangerous and advised the author to correct the defects, which Greene politely refused to do. Cardinal Griffin of Westminster asked him not to allow reprints of translations of *The Power and the Glory* without making appropriate corrections. Rome complained that the book emphasized man's "wretchedness" and "portrayed a state of affairs so paradoxical and erroneous that it would disconcert an unenlightened person."[76]

Further, the Holy Office complained that the book displayed an "abnormal propensity towards situations in which one kind of sexual immorality or another plays a role." Vatican officials suggested that Greene should be informed that "literature of this kind does harm to the cause of the true religion" and that "in the future he should behave more cautiously."[77] They insisted that the novel "posed a danger to the virtue of the majority" because of its "odd and paradoxical" views. Greene replied, "The aim of the book was to oppose the power of the sacraments and the indestructibility of the church on the one hand with, on the other, the merely temporal power of an essentially Communist state."[78] In fact, the novel highlights the resilience of the church in the face of persecution.

Cardinal Montini, then in the Vatican Secretariat of State but who was to become Pope Paul VI in 1963, took a more balanced view of Greene's book. He said, "I have no objection to make to the just observations in the [censure of] this work. But it seems to me that, in such a judgment, there is lacking a sense of the work's

75. Bergonzi, *Study in Greene*, 137.
76. "How Rome Tried to Censor Greene's Masterpiece," para. 9.
77. "How Rome Tried to Censor Greene's Masterpiece," para. 12.
78. McHale, "Graham Greene's Pope," 22.

substantial merits." He also pointed to the "heroic fidelity to his own ministry within the innermost soul of a priest who is in many respects reprehensible." Thus, while the Holy Office was critical of the novel, Pope Paul VI, who had read the book himself, told Greene, "Some aspects of your books are certain to offend some Catholics, but you should pay no attention to that."[79]

*The Power and the Glory* has been regarded as Greene's finest work. Perhaps certain aspects of the book might be offensive to some pious Catholics, as Paul VI pointed out. It might be the intention of the author to jolt believers out of their complacency and comfort zone. However, in Greene's story, we follow the journey of a sinner and saint, the story of sin and salvation, feeling the struggle, doubt, and final resolution. The whisky priest's path of sainthood is marked by fear, temptation, and betrayal as he attempts to escape persecution by the state. The appearance of another priest at the end signifies resurrection and the triumph of Christianity—for thine is the kingdom, the power, and the glory. This novel reflects Greene's understanding of human existence as essentially infernal and his conviction that the only way to peace and happiness is to follow the vision of God.

79. Quoted in McHale, "Graham Greene's Pope," 22.

Chapter 7

# Apostate or Apostle in *Silence*?

BORN IN TOKYO, SHUSAKU Endo (1923–96), grew up in Japanese-occupied Manchuria. After his parents' divorce, Endo returned to Japan with his mother in 1933, and through her influence and that of his aunt, was baptized as a Catholic in 1934 at the age of eleven. He described his Christian faith as ill-fitting clothes that shaped his literary work. Graduated from Keio University with a bachelor's degree in French literature in 1949, Endo travelled to France to read Catholic fiction at the University of Lyon. As a novelist, he explored the relationship between East and West through a Christian perspective. Among the body of fiction he wrote, *Silence*, published in 1966, is his masterpiece. It was made into a movie in 2016 directed by Martin Scorsese.

Like Graham Greene's *The Power and the Glory* which narrates the story of a fugitive priest, set in Mexico in the early twentieth century, the context of Shusaku Endo's *Silence* is the persecution of Christian missionaries in seventeenth-century Japan with a focus on the Portuguese Jesuit Fr. Sebastian Rodrigues. Through the first-person epistolary narrative, the author delves into the inner turmoil of the priest as he struggles between his evangelizing zeal and his condescending attitude towards the natives he is ministering to. In fact, he wonders if the people whose souls he is trying to save really understand the teachings of the church. After his apostasy, Rodrigues attempts to justify himself by reflecting on the life of Christ in relation to his downfall and failed mission, claiming that he has renounced the church as an institution, but not his faith.

In this chapter, we will explore Endo's nuanced portrayal of the priest Rodrigues and the transformation of his religious belief into a more authentic faith in the suffering Jesus. Stripped of his pride and colonial mentality, Rodrigues undergoes humiliation and shame in the public renunciation of Christianity. This paradoxically turns the priest from the "apostate Paul" to being more like the apostle Peter. The dramatization of the violent persecution of foreign missionaries and Japanese faithful is based on historical facts and modelled on real-life figures.

## Jesuit Mission in Japan

St. Francis Xavier, the great Jesuit missionary, arrived in Kagoshima in 1549 to propagate the faith. Within fifty years, about three hundred thousand natives had been baptized. The Christian mission adopted a Western approach, politically and culturally, and were part of the European maritime expansion. Initially, the Japanese feudal lords (*daimyo*) wanted to have commercial ties with Western nations and thus allowed the entry of missionaries and tolerated their presence. However, the unification of Japan under a central government was accompanied by a growing suspicious of foreigners. The Tokugawa shogunate (1603–1867) sought to promote a strong nationalist spirit by politically unifying the various warring states. Christianity was perceived as interfering with Japanese internal affairs, disrupting and undermining the central authority under the ruling family.

The Japanese authorities began to feel that "Christianity was a disease which infected their subjects with disloyalty." Christianity was formally banned in 1614, when Shogun Tokugawa Ieyasu revoked the policies of toleration with the Edict of Expulsion. It accused the Christians of attempting "to make Japan into 'their own possession' . . . [and] to 'contravene government regulations, traduce Shinto, calumniate the True Law, destroy righteousness, corrupt goodness'—in short, to subvert the native Japanese, the Buddhist, and the Confucian foundations of the social order."[1] It also set the stage for the persecution of Christians. More than four thousand Japanese Christians were killed between 1597 and 1650 by mass crucifixion and later through the "pit."

Christian missionaries, especially the Portuguese and Spanish, who had arrived in the middle of the sixteenth century, were expelled. It is significant to note that only Catholic missionaries, like the Jesuits, were expelled by the shogunate, but not the Dutch traders. "Portuguese ships were forbidden to enter the harbors of Japan."[2] Presumably, the Dutch merchants were keen only to trade and looked upon the Portuguese as rivals.

When the crackdown began, Christians were asked to step on an embossed copper image of Jesus in a procedure known as *fumie*. The trampling on Christ's face was ritualized with a public denunciation of the Christian faith and was an annual event for many native faithful during the early Edo period.[3] Those who refused were tortured and killed, some by being hung upside down in a pit filled with excrement, slowly bleeding to death through a tiny slit incurred on their temples and foreheads. Others were boiled alive in the water of Mt. Unzen Jigoku or crucified at sea. Setting the novel within this historical context leads to multiple interpretations—is Rodrigues's apostasy a denunciation of faith or a perfection of Christian virtue?

## The Story of *Silence*

*Silence* narrates the journey of the Jesuit Sebastian Rodrigues, who travels to Japan secretly in the mid-seventeenth century. He goes to the various islands to minister to the *kakure kirishitan* (hidden Christians), who are forced to hide because of brutal persecution.

1. Quoted in Netland, "Encountering Christ," 167.
2. Endo, *Silence*, 31.
3. Wachal, "Forbidden Ships to Chartered Tours," 99.

It is also Rodrigues's mission to search for Christovao Ferreira, his mentor and the former Jesuit provincial, who is reported as missing. Ferreira was, in fact, a key figure in the early Jesuit mission to Japan. When his letters stopped abruptly, Ferreira was believed to have apostatized under torture by the Japanese authorities. News of his apostasy was reported in Europe. It affected the morale of the mission as well as of the local faithful, who went into hiding.

With the help of a weak-willed Japanese, Kichijiro, whom he encounters in Macau, Rodrigues and another Jesuit, Francisco Garrpe, arrive on one of the islands of Japan. Witnessing the cruel persecution and immense sufferings of the Japanese faithful, Rodrigues is angered by the silence of God. To comfort himself, he imagines a lovely blue-eyed face of Christ as he endures physical and mental anguish in a land that he thinks is hostile, foreboding, and unforgiving. The inhospitality of Japan arises from its harsh terrain as well as from the samurai and their leader, the notorious Inoue, the "architect of Christian persecution."[4] The Buddhist bonzes are also hostile towards the Christian missionaries.

Betrayed by Kichijiro for three hundred pieces of silver and handed over to the authorities, Rodrigues meets his old mentor in a poignant scene where Ferreira confirms the rumors of his apostasy as true. His action, he explains, was motivated by compassion, not cowardice. It was love and mercy for the Japanese faithful who were being tortured and executed. Just by waving his hand to signal his apostasy, the captured Christians were spared. Ferreira believes this painful decision was an act of faith, hope, and charity, which would be condemned by the church, but would be commended by Christ himself.

Shocked and disappointed by his teacher's betrayal, Rodrigues soon finds himself in the same predicament. Witnessing the sufferings of the *kakure kirishitan*, staring at the still image of Jesus placed by the authorities for him to trample, he sees only a dirty and stained portrait, not the blue-eyed face of Christ that he had imagined. In this confrontation, where his imagination

4. Endo, *Silence*, 36.

clashes with the stark reality, Jesus speaks out, thus breaking this unbearable silence. Endo writes:

> The priest raises his foot. In it he feels a dull, heavy pain. This is no mere formality. He will now trample on what he has considered the most beautiful thing in his life, on what he has believed most pure, on what is filled with the ideals and the dreams of man. How his foot aches! And then the Christ in bronze speaks to the priest: "Trample! Trample! I more than anyone know of the pain in your foot. Trample! It was to be trampled by men that I was born into this world. It was to share men's pain that I carried my cross."[5]

Van C. Gessel points out that the voice from the *fumie* does not give a command but rather an utterance filled with love and forgiveness. It is a voice that encourages the priest to step on the copper plate so that the suffering of others may be ended and his own as well. This voice is thus "a maternal one, not the stern voice of a judgmental Father but the merciful, accepting whisper of a deity willing to forgive."[6]

## The Changing Face of Christ

Endo explains that "the most meaningful thing in the novel is the change in the hero's image of Christ."[7] For him, the theme of the story lies in the changing face of Jesus, and not the transformation of the protagonist. In Rodrigues's childhood,

> The face of Christ had been for him the fulfillment of his every dream and ideal. . . . Even in its moments of terrible torture this face had never lost its beauty. Those soft, clear eyes which pierced to the very core of a man's being were now fixed upon him. . . . When the vision of this face came before him, fear and trembling seemed to

5. Endo, *Silence*, 271.
6. Gessel, "Hearing God in Silence," 161.
7. Quoted in Keuss, "Lenten Face of Christ," 274.

vanish like the tiny ripples that are quietly sucked up by
the sand of the sea-shore.[8]

This beautiful vision of Christ eventually changes into something less consoling as Rodrigues experiences spiritual anguish
and imprisonment. Witnessing the Japanese Christians stepping
on the *fumie*, he sees "the face of Christ, wet with tears. When
the gentle eyes looked straight into his, the priest was filled with
shame."[9]

As a child, Rodrigues viewed Jesus as a triumphant savior,
one who performs miracles, heals the sick, and comforts the sinners. Now, faced with torture and pain, he sees the suffering Christ,
and experiences profound sadness. The face that he tramples on
when he apostatizes is no longer the blue-eyed Jesus of victorious
Western Christianity, but "the ugly face of Christ, crowned with
thorns and the thin, outstretched arms."[10] As he steps on the image, the face tells him, "Trample! It was to be trampled on by men
that I was born into this world!"[11] This transformation of the face
of Christ from beautiful and consoling to hideous and battered
suggests a more profound understanding of the Christian faith on
the part of the priest. It is a more authentic faith stripped of much
of his self-conceit and delusion.

Rodrigues has always been "fascinated by the face of Christ
just like a man fascinated by the face of his beloved" because the
Scriptures make no mention of it.[12] Given his desire to see the face
of Jesus, it is poignant that his captors demand that he steps on
the *fumie*, the embossed image of Christ. Not only is he able to
see the face of the suffering Christ, but he also hears his voice too:
"Trample! Trample!"[13] The irony is that Rodrigues fulfills his spiri-

8. Endo, *Silence*, 170.

9. Endo, *Silence*, 189.

10. Endo, *Silence*, 270.

11. Endo, *Silence*, 271.

12. Endo, *Silence*, 47.

13. Endo, *Silence*, 271.

tual longing, to see the face of Christ and to hear him, by literally stepping on Jesus's image and publicly denouncing him.

The changing face of Christ in Rodrigues's vision, as he enters Japan, enduring hardship and imprisonment, is Endo's attempt to accommodate Christianity, a Western faith, to Japanese sensibilities. Endo stresses the humanity of Jesus, the suffering servant, because Japanese religious minds have "little tolerance for any kind of transcendent being who judges humans harshly, then punishes them."[14] Japanese prefer a maternal religion that is tolerant, allowing human weaknesses, rather than the strict paternalistic faith that Western Christianity portrays. Thus, in his writings, Endo attempts to depict Christianity like a sympathetic mother rather than a harsh father.

Apostasy is a serious sin in Catholic teaching, but Endo sees it as an entry into a new form of faith, without Western trappings, accommodated to the local Japanese cultural imagination.[15] This transformation takes place when Rodrigues witnesses the torture of the Japanese, which eventually leads him to step on the *fumie*. While reflecting on his apostasy, he sees the face of Jesus telling him, "I was not silent. I suffered beside you."[16]

Endo's understanding of the gospel is a Jesus that is in solidarity with the poor and oppressed, at odds with the rich and powerful. It is a Christ that participates in human vulnerability and weakness. In *Silence*, Christianity appears as a failed religion, just as Jesus is considered a failure, rejected, and killed by his own people. The faith, however, remains because it is in the participation in human sufferings that one can overcome human shortcomings.

14. Quoted in Wachal, "Forbidden Ships to Chartered Tours," 100–101.
15. Wachal, "Forbidden Ships to Chartered Tours," 102.
16. Endo, *Silence*, 297.

## Masculine and Feminine

The two faces of Christ imagined by Rodrigues symbolize the two aspects of Christianity.[17] The masculine face of Jesus, "filled with vigor and strength," attracts Rodrigues before he apostatizes.[18] This masculine or paternal side of Christianity, the Christ of Christendom, relates to European expansionism. When news of Ferreira's apostasy reaches Europe, it was not simply a failure of one individual priest, but "a humiliating defeat for the faith itself and for the whole of Europe."[19]

In other words, the "European ego" has been damaged, and it is the responsibility of Rodrigues to restore that ego in Japan and to save souls.[20] This kind of paternalistic approach is detrimental to the whole missionary enterprise in the East. In reality, Rodrigues's zeal to evangelize the Japanese is to satisfy his own ambition. The interpreter bluntly tells Rodrigues, "Father, have you thought of the suffering you have inflicted on many peasants just because of your dream, just because you want to impose your selfish dream upon Japan?"[21]

The feminine aspect is in the Jesus that suffers, "the ugly face of Christ, crowned with thorns" that is exposed to the priest after he steps on the *fumie*.[22] Rodrigues realizes that these two aspects are found in the one Jesus. His experience in Japan affirms that if the faith is to flourish, the feminine side of Jesus must be fostered. This insight seems to narrow the gulf between Western Christianity and Japanese sensibilities as the suffering Jesus manages to take root in Japanese mud swamp in a way that a victorious Christ could not.

Endo's preference for a maternalistic Christianity was influenced by the Buddhist concept of mercy, which forgives everything,

17. Ho, "*Silence* and the Japanization of Christianity," 74.
18. Endo, *Silence*, 47.
19. Endo, *Silence*, 26.
20. Ho, "*Silence* and the Japanization of Christianity," 74.
21. Endo, *Silence*, 218.
22. Endo, *Silence*, 270.

even the sins of the apostate, which a Father God would perhaps not. The image of Christ that Endo embraces is one possessing the "maternal capacity to forgive the faults of traitors."[23] Not a powerful person who performs miracles, but one who accompanies people in their sufferings and weeps with the weak and dying.

## Clash of Eastern Culture and Western Creed

The dialogue between Rodrigues and the Japanese magistrate Inoue sets the stage for Endo to dramatize the conflict between Japanese culture and Western Christianity. Inoue refers to Japan as a "swamp" that will eventually destroy Christianity from within. Once the missionaries are gone, the Japanese believers will distort the Christian faith, he asserts. There are still some Christian farmers remaining on the remote islands of Goto and Ikitsuki. But Inoue has no desire to pursue them; he says, "If the root is cut, the sapling withers and the leaves die. The proof of this is that the God whom the peasants of Goto and Ikitsuki secretly serve has gradually changed so as to be no longer like the Christian God at all."[24]

Inoue, who was earlier baptized for the sake of promotion, challenges Christianity's claim to universality and believes that eventually Japanese culture will overwhelm this Western import, syncretizing and modifying it. In fact, Rodrigues already has misgivings about the compatibility of Japanese beliefs and Christianity. In his letters, Rodrigues complains about the excessive adoration of icons by Japanese and that "the peasants sometimes seem to honor Mary rather than Christ."[25] At the same time, he realizes that his presence poses a great danger to them and increases their sufferings.

It is Christovao Ferreira, the former Jesuit provincial, who has apostatized and collaborated with the Japanese authorities, who proves the rationality of Inoue's argument. Ferreira presents

23. Quoted in McEntire, "Confessions of 'the Weak,'" 168.
24. Endo, *Silence*, 293–94.
25. Endo, *Silence*, 98.

himself as "an old missionary defeated by missionary work."[26] Ferreira apostatized to save the lives of five Japanese peasants who were hanging in the pit together with him for three days. "Certainly, Christ would have apostatized for them," he reasons.[27] Ferreira apostatizes also to break the unbearable silence of God in the midst of so much pain and suffering.

When Ferreira claims that Christianity cannot take root in Japanese soil, Rodrigues argues that it is because the roots are torn up. Ferreira merely responds by saying, "This country is a more terrible swamp than you can imagine. Whenever you plant a sapling in this swamp the roots begin to rot; the leaves grow yellow and wither. And we have planted the sapling of Christianity in this swamp."[28] Ferreira says that the swamp has distorted the nature of Christianity, and the God the converts worshipped is not the God taught by the church: "What the Japanese of that time believed in was not our God. It was their own gods. For a long time we failed to realize this and firmly believed they had become Christians."[29]

## Self-Deception and Insecurities

The psychological pressure inflicted upon Rodrigues makes his act of apostasy understandable. Unlike the Japanese Christians in the pit, Rodrigues is not being tortured, and thus he sounds naive or even hypocritical when he says that the peasants who are being tortured and executed will receive heavenly rewards. Ferreira accuses Rodrigues of self-deception, disguising his own insecurities with beautiful banalities; preoccupied with his own salvation, he has placed his interests above others, refusing to save the Japanese from suffering out of fear of betraying the church.

This indictment strikes deep into Rodrigues's pride— he is named by his former superior to be a coward, afraid of

26. Endo, *Silence*, 236.
27. Endo, *Silence*, 268.
28. Endo, *Silence*, 237.
29. Endo, *Silence*, 237–38.

self-abnegation. Ferreira continues, "You dread to be the dregs of the Church, like me. . . . Yet I was the same as you. On that cold, black night I, too, was as you are now. And yet is your way of acting love? A priest ought to live in imitation of Christ. If Christ were here . . . ."[30] The emotional impact of Ferreira's words on Rodrigues is devastating, "the apostasy comes to seem inevitable . . . as the result of the accumulative effective power of the portrait of the protagonist's moral dispositions."[31]

The defeat of Ferreira strengthens Inoue's argument regarding the incompatibility between Christianity and the Japanese mindset. To convince Rodrigues to apostatize, Ferreira claims that the success of the early Christian mission was in fact an illusion because the Japanese eventually distorted their newfound faith. To prove his cynical viewpoint, he comments, "From the beginning those same Japanese who confused 'Deus' and 'Dainichi' twisted and changed our God and began to create something different."[32] God is lost in translation.

Ferreira and Inoue tell Rodrigues that holding on to his religion is an illusion, an escapism, a refusal to accept current political realities. Religious faith, they suggest, is essentially a subjective experience with no connection to objective realities. Ferreira further argues that his apostasy is merely a show, an external act, which implies that his faith is still intact. Rodrigues's tenacious clinging to his faith only endangers the lives of the Japanese faithful. To apostatize in such a situation is really an act of compassion and mercy, which Ferreira has done. Netland puts it this way, "The command to apostatize comes not primarily as an invitation to escape suffering, but paradoxically as an appeal to his deepest Christian values. What is more Christ-like than to lay down one's life for others?"[33]

---

30. Endo, *Silence*, 268.
31. Washburn, "Is Abjection a Virtue?" 209.
32. Endo, *Silence*, 239.
33. Netland, "Encountering Christ," 172.

## Conversion of Rodrigues

Portrayed as a person anxious to prove his fidelity to the Jesuit mission, Rodrigues's motive is also to dispel the rumor of Ferreira's apostasy, or "to offer himself as atonement for the appalling offense of his mentor's apostasy."[34] His early letters reveal his spiritual pride, his desire for martyrdom, as he reflects with fear and fascination on the danger of his journey. However, when he arrives in Japan, his view of martyrdom changes.

> I had long read about martyrdom in the lives of the saints—how the souls of the martyrs had gone home to Heaven, how they had been filled with glory in Paradise, how the angels had blown trumpets. This was the splendid martyrdom I had often seen in my dreams. But the martyrdom of the Japanese Christians I now describe to you was no such glorious thing. What a miserable and painful business it was![35]

Filled with ambition and pride, Rodrigues's motivation for martyrdom is misplaced because in the Catholic tradition one cannot deliberately seek it; martyrdom is thrust upon the person. Those who actively seek the road to martyrdom are not seeking it for the glory of God, but for their own glory. This is contrary to the motto of the Jesuits, *Ad majorem Dei gloriam*: "for the greater glory of God." Thus, Rodrigues's vision of martyrdom is misdirected and distorted. Another kind of martyrdom, however, awaits Rodrigues—the death of his Christian identity and moral certainty.[36]

In *Silence*, we also witness the gradual transformation of Rodrigues through his dealings with the weakling Kichijiro, who betrays him. We witness the conversion in Rodrigues through his encounter with those who control him, like the magistrate Inoue and his former teacher Ferreira, who persuade him to apostatize by trampling on the image of Christ. The story can be simply summarized as "the transformation of the moral dispositions of an

34. Bosco, "Charting Endo's Catholic Literary Aesthetic," 85.

35. Endo, *Silence*, 103–4.

36. Cavanaugh, "God of Silence," 12.

individual who, when placed in extreme circumstances, is forced to behave in ways contradictory to the very modes of thought and feeling that ground his self-conception and identity."[37]

In other words, Rodrigues's faith is purified when stripped of Western colonial privileges and personal vanity. His missionary fervor is tempered by a more authentic Christian discipleship. As the Japanese authorities attempt to eliminate Christianity completely, the priest finds the faith in the presence of those tortured and executed. When Rodrigues performs "the most painful act of love that has ever been performed,"[38] he realizes that "my lord is different from the God that is preached in the churches."[39] Not stained by Western arrogance anymore, the priest finds the faith of the Japanese Catholics more edifying and purer.

Stepping on the *fumie* is not just a mere formality, even though one of the officials urges Rodrigues, "I'm not telling you to trample with sincerity and conviction. This is only a formality. Just putting your foot on the thing won't hurt your convictions."[40] The interpreter also attempts to convince Rodrigues, "Only go through with the exterior form of trampling."[41] After his apostasy, the Portuguese Jesuit is given a Japanese name, Okada San'emon, given a Japanese wife, and affiliated to a Buddhist temple. But there is an indication that, deep inside, he has not changed his religious convictions. The *Diary* records that he is "engaged in writing a disavowal of his religion" a few times.[42] Rodrigues must live his faith in silence, as demanded by his captors, in a society that disdains the public proclamation of a foreign religion. Faith, in *Silence*, is revealed as more than a personal belief; it illuminates how one's faith affects the lives of others as well.

37. Washburn, "Is Abjection a Virtue?" 207.

38. Endo, *Silence*, 269–70.

39. Endo, *Silence*, 276.

40. Endo, *Silence*, 190.

41. Endo, *Silence*, 271.

42. Endo, *Silence*, 300.

## *Kenosis*: Self-Emptying

The sacrifice of Jesus is an expression of God's presence and love. Through the emptying of his life, *kenosis*, Jesus enables the person to witness the depth of God's love. *Kenosis* is the self-emptying of one's own will to align it with God's will. It is the expression of Jesus's humility, of one who relinquishes all his powers of divinity (Phil 2:6–8). Rodrigues, out of compassion for the Japanese Christians, also empties himself by stepping on the *fumie* against his will.

Salvation occurs when we are called upon to share in the likeness of God, becoming like Christ, a broken body as well as a glorified one. In the same way, by trampling on the *fumie*, Rodrigues strips away his sense of pride and self-sufficiency. His transformation occurs in the realization that God shares in his agony and anguish. Rodrigues, the priest, imitates Christ, through his pain and sorrow in the act of apostasy, a manifestation of mercy for the Japanese people. Netland writes, "The apparent defeat of Christianity by the mudswamp of Japan ironically validates the very Kingdom it seeks to destroy. It is the moral authority of the suffering Christ that confirms Rodrigues' act."[43] In *Silence*, we witness how the love of God is revealed in the suffering of human existence.

## Affirmation of Faith

After stepping on the *fumie*, Rodrigues regards Kichijiro with a mixture of disgust and empathy. He sadly realizes that there is not much difference between him and this weakling. In fact, it is Kichijiro who leads Rodrigues to struggle with the silence of God when he utters, "Why had Deus Sama imposed this suffering upon us? . . . [W]hat evil have we done?"[44] The words of this coward pierce the heart of Rodrigues like a sharp needle, which moves him to ask, "Why has our Lord imposed this torture and this persecution on poor Japanese peasants? No, Kichijiro was trying to

43. Netland, "Encountering Christ," 172.
44. Endo, *Silence*, 96.

express something different, something even more sickening. The silence of God."[45]

Kichijiro returns to Rodrigues for confession even after the priest has apostatized. He tells Rodrigues, "In this world are the strong and the weak. The strong never yield to torture, and they go to Paradise; but what about those, like myself, who are born weak?"[46] In spite of his weakness and failure, Kichijiro returns to his faith repeatedly, which "signifies the presence of grace" in his human weakness.[47] This discernment is fully played out in Rodrigues's own journey. Agreeing to hear his confession although it is dangerous and forbidden, Rodrigues says to Kichijiro, "There are neither the strong nor the weak. Can anyone say that the weak do not suffer more than the strong?"[48]

It is in our weakness that God reveals his grace. When St. Paul asks the Lord to remove the thorn in his flesh, the answer is, "My grace is sufficient for you, for power is made perfect in weakness" (2 Cor 12:9). Endo portrays the affirmation of faith in the most paradoxical way, an apostate priest hearing the confession of his betrayer.

## Parallel to Peter

The reference to the cock crow immediately after the betrayal suggests that Rodrigues would be like Peter, weeping bitterly (Matt 26:75), shedding tears of repentance, and being reconciled to Christ eventually. In fact, the fall and rise of Rodrigues appears to parallel that of Peter's relationship to his master. Like Peter, the priest understands the teaching of Jesus more deeply after his denial. Experiencing remorse, Rodrigues is also able to forgive Kichijiro and is confident that God has forgiven him. This

---

45. Endo, *Silence*, 96.

46. Endo, *Silence*, 296–97.

47. Bosco, "Charting Endo's Catholic Literary Aesthetic," 85.

48. Endo, *Silence*, 297–98.

transformation of Rodrigues parallels the conversion we witness in Peter in the Gospel.

Although Rodrigues has lost his status in the church as a priest, he has not lost his standing with Christ as a Christian. In fact, he continues to stand up for Christ after his public apostasy. In others words, like Peter, he falls and stands up. Thus, Rodrigues is more of an apostle than an apostate. It is significant to note that the Japanese word used by Endo for apostasy in the novel is *korobu*, a word without religious connotation. It literally means "to trip and fall," implying that the fallen person will rise again.[49]

The act of trampling on Jesus's image reminds us of Jesus's presence, as we hear him telling Rodrigues, "I was not silent. I suffered beside you."[50] Thus, the act of apostasy is an affirmation of faith, a belief in the existence of God. Apostasy is not a sin in this context. What is sin then? Inside his prison cell, Rodrigues can hear the guards chattering. These "were men . . . indifferent to the fate of others. . . . Sin, he reflected, is not to steal and tell lies. Sin is for one man to walk brutally over the life of another and to be quite oblivious of the wounds he has left behind."[51]

Rodrigues's conversion when he hears the voice of Christ and tramples upon his image indicates a transformation of the priest's heart, from chauvinism to charity. As prophet Ezekiel says, "A new heart I will give you, and a new spirit I will put within you; and I will remove from your body the heart of stone and give you a heart of flesh" (Ezek 36:26). Endo was convinced that the uncompromising and masculine nature of Christianity does not appeal to the Japanese, who prefer motherly and feminine deities.[52] Freed from his understanding of the church as a paternalistic taskmaster, Rodrigues now embraces a faith that is more compassionate and merciful.

We could argue that if Rodrigues refused to apostatize, the peasants would be tortured to death and thus achieve martyrdom.

49. Gessel, "*Silence* on Opposite Shores," 34.
50. Endo, *Silence*, 297.
51. Endo, *Silence*, 144.
52. Gessel, "*Silence* on Opposite Shores," 34.

This would foil the plan of Inoue, who fully understands the teaching of Tertullian: "The blood of the martyrs is the seed of the church." This refusal would give witness that God and not the magistrate is in control. The magistrate would then have no power over the life and death of his prisoners. The death of the three peasants in the pit could be seen in the light of the death and resurrection of Christ.[53] But the peasants have already apostatized and thus, Rodrigues's stepping on the *fumie* is an affirmation of faith in a forgiving God. Alive, the priest, like Peter, is able to obey Jesus's command to "take care of my sheep" (John 21:16).

---

53. Cavanaugh, "Absolute Moral Norms and Human Suffering," 114.

# Conclusion

IN THIS WORK WE have witnessed how the protagonist attains sanctity through different kinds of suffering. In his second letter to the Corinthians, Paul expressed his contentment in facing various challenges and difficulties for the sake of Christ, acknowledging that in moments of weakness, he found strength. This unique concept of strength being derived from vulnerability is a distinguishing characteristic of Christianity. It suggests that when a person recognizes their own vulnerabilities, they are more open to and dependent on God. Through surrendering oneself to God, one can find strength to overcome all challenges and difficulties (2 Cor 12:9–11).

The redemptive power of suffering acknowledged by Christians helps individuals identify with Christ's passion. Suffering brings a person closer to God and others, leading to their sanctification, to the process of becoming holy. This work explores the portrayal of priests in history and literature, examining their struggles and sufferings as they live out their vocation, ministering to their flock in various social, cultural, and political contexts. Their sufferings include physical, emotional, and spiritual anguish. Since the priests are portrayed as fallible beings but capable of transcending their human limitations and weaknesses, this work also emphasizes the transformative power of grace. Through their suffering and pain, the priests develop and cultivate the virtues of love, forgiveness, and tolerance.

In spite of the negative news regarding clerical conduct in recent years, I would like to testify that many priests are struggling to live up to their calling with fidelity and love. They are the movers and shakers in their communities, and their lives make a difference for those fortunate to encounter them. While not many have suffered as much as the priests narrated in these chapters or lived such heroic lives, I would like to share the personal experience of someone I have known for years, Father Bonifacio Solís, OP, my former superior in the Dominican Order. He is the epic representation of the very committed and dedicated priests we have in the church.

When I heard Father Solís had returned to Spain for good, I felt sad and found it hard to believe. Now he has left this world, and I am devastated. I never had the chance nor the courage to tell him how much I loved and admired him. I am very grateful to him for sending me to Seville for the novitiate and to Rome to study for the priesthood. He gave me his blessings when I requested to join the Diocese of Hong Kong and wrote to Pope Francis regarding my incardination into the diocese.

Father Solís was one of those larger-than-life figures many of us only read about in books or see in movies. A first-class administrator and a dedicated priest, he was elected as the provincial superior of the Rosary Province for four terms—which was rather challenging and detrimental to his health. Marvelously talented and gifted with relating to people, he was admired by many peers and followers in Asia and Europe. I used to think that if he had not been a priest, he would have been president or CEO of a global corporation. If he had been married, he would have been a fantastic father to his children. As a priest, he gave his whole heart in all his duties and religious life—total dedication and without consideration for his comfort or convenience.

Father Solís deeply loved the Dominican Order and the church, which could be exhausting. Convinced of the mission, he pushed himself to his limits at great cost to his well-being. On the surface, he appeared stern and aloof, but we all knew that deep inside, he was a gentle soul, a lovely person. He was always there for his brothers.

As a provincial, he had to travel extensively and frequently, which I think he loved. As a humble servant of God, he always took the cheapest route despite great inconvenience. While in transit or waiting for the next flight, he would do correspondence and proofread or edit the papers and theses of student-brothers. Whether at home or traveling in Asia, Europe, or Latin America, he always promptly replied to emails. At a Provincial Chapter in Avila on our day off, Father Solís would borrow his sister's car to visit the parents of friars working abroad.

I never saw him take a holiday—he was happiest at work. He ate and drank sparingly and was always present for prayers and spiritual exercises. When he stepped down as provincial, he took over the task of novice master with great fidelity. I thought it would be tough on him without the perks of high position and the freedom of mobility! But no, he did very well—he exemplified his vows.

A valuable yet seldom mentioned talent is Fr. Solís's skill in solving canonical issues regarding the many religious who, for one reason or another, were living in irregular situations. He once said that a good religious does not need a superior and showed us this through his everyday life.

Highly intelligent, Father Solís picked up new responsibilities and other duties as the province syndic [bursar] very quickly— even when he was seventy. He was trained at the Alphonsianum in Rome, graduating with a doctorate in moral theology, and he could teach almost anything. A man of that caliber would succeed in any profession, whether in the church or in civil life.

Father Solís had a soft spot for the Chinese and was very focused on promoting vocations in China. He once told the Dominicans in Australia that if he were to start all over again, he would learn Chinese. He had great love and sincere respect for the Chinese people.

Father Solís is in heaven praying for us. Of that I am convinced. But the pain of his absence will always be felt by us. He once said he would like to go quickly when the time came. Our merciful God has granted his faithful servant, Father Solís, his wish. The world is a much poorer place without him, and we all must work doubly hard to fill his big space.

Father Bonifacio Garcia Solis of the Order of Preachers died in Oviedo, Spain, on October 23, 2021. He was seventy-six. May his soul rest in peace.

# Bibliography

Americas Watch Committee. *El Salvador's Decade of Terror: Human Rights Since the Assassination of Archbishop Romero*. Human Rights Watch Books. New Haven: Yale University Press, 1991.

Arrupe, Pedro. "A New Service to the World of Today." *Mid-Stream* 20 (1981) 374–84.

———. *One Jesuit's Spiritual Journey: Autobiographical Conversations with Jean-Paul Dietsch, SJ*. Translated by Ruth Bradley. St. Louis: Institute of Jesuit Sources, 1986.

Baldridge, Cates. *Graham Greene's Fictions: The Virtues of Extremity*. Columbia: University of Missouri Press, 2000.

Barany, Zoltan. "Building National Armies After Civil War: Lessons from Bosnia, El Salvador, and Lebanon." *Political Science Quarterly* 129 (2014) 211–38.

Baum, Gregory. *Man Becoming: God in Secular Experience*. New York: Seabury, 1979.

Bayley, Elisabeth. "The Conflict of Legends and the Corrective Lens of Love in Willa Cather's *Death Comes for the Archbishop*: A Girardian Analysis." *Heythrop Journal* 54 (2013) 835–45.

Baym, Nina. *Women Writers of the American West, 1833–1927*. Urbana: University of Illinois Press, 2011.

Bergonzi, Bernard. *A Study in Greene: Graham Greene and the Art of the Novel*. Oxford: Oxford University Press, 2008.

Bernanos, George. *Diary of a Country Priest*. Translated by Pamela Morris. Cambridge: Da Capo, 2002.

Block, Ed. "Friendship, Renunciation, and a Celebration of the Transcendent Self: Willa Cather's *Death Comes for the Archbishop* After One Hundred Years." *Renascence* 73 (2021) 197–219.

Bloom, Edward A., and Lillian D. Bloom. "The Genesis of *Death Comes for the Archbishop*." *American Literature* 26 (1955) 479–506.

Boff, Leonardo. *Liberating Grace*. Maryknoll, NY: Orbis, 1984.

———. "Martyrdom: An Attempt at Systematic Reflection." *Concilium* 163 (1983) 12–17.

Bohlke, L. Brent. "Willa Cather's Nebraska Priests and *Death Comes for the Archbishop*." *Great Plains Quarterly* 4 (1984) 264–69.

Bosco, Mark. "Charting Endo's Catholic Literary Aesthetic." In *Approaching Silence: New Perspectives on Shusaku Endo's Classic Novel*, edited by Mark W. Dennis and Darren J. N. Middleton, 77–92. London: Bloomsbury Academic, 2015.

———. "From *The Power and the Glory* to *The Honorary Consul*: The Development of Graham Greene's Catholic Imagination." *Religion & Literature* 36 (2004) 51–74.

Brockett, Charles. "El Salvador: The Long Journey from Violence to Reconciliation." *Latin American Research Review* 29 (1994) 174–87.

Brockman, James R. *Romero: A Life*. Maryknoll, NY: Orbis, 1989.

Burke, Kevin F. *Pedro Arrupe: Essential Writings*. Maryknoll, NY: Orbis, 2004.

Campbell-Johnston, Michael. "Pedro Arrupe Remembered." *The Way* 51 (2012) 77–89.

The Cardinal Kung Foundation. "Biography." http://www.cardinalkung foundation.org/ck/CKlife.php.

Caritas Australia. "Saint Oscar Romero Biography." https://www.caritas.org.au/ resources/school-resources/oscar-romero-biography/.

Cather, Willa. *Death Comes for the Archbishop*. New York: Knopf, 1955.

Catholic World Report. "A Profile in Courage: Cardinal Kung and Catholic Resistance in Shanghai." September 8, 2023. https://www.catholicworldreport.com/2023/09/08/profile-courage-cardinal-kung-catholic-resistance-shanghai/.

Cavanaugh, William T. "Absolute Moral Norms and Human Suffering: An Apocalyptic Reading of Endo's *Silence*." *Logos* 2 (1999) 96–116.

———. "The God of Silence." *Commonweal* 125 (1998): 10–12.

Christiansen, Drew. "Catholic Peacemaking, 1991–2005: The Legacy of John Paul II." *Review of Faith & International Affairs* 4 (2006) 21–28.

Cloete, Nettie. "Religious Paradoxes in Graham Greene's Novels." *Koers* 63 (1998) 313–25.

Closkey, Pilar Hogan, and John P. Hogan. "Introduction: Romero's Vision and the City Parish—Urban Ministry and Urban Planning." In *Romero's Legacy: The Call to Peace and Justice*, edited by Pilar Hogan Closkey and John P. Hogan, 1–14. Lanham, MD: Rowman & Littlefield, 2007.

Coles, Robert. "The Pilgrimage of George Bernanos—'The Supreme Grace Would Be to Love Ourselves.'" *New York Times*, June 8, 1986. https://www.nytimes.com/1986/06/08/books/the-pilgrimage-of-george-bernanos-the-supreme-grave-would-be-to-love-ourselves.html.

Darring, Gerald. "1971 Synod of Bishops Justice in the World—Critical Comments Selected." *JustMeCatholicFaith*, August 19, 2012. https://justmecatholicfaith.wordpress.com/2012/08/19/1971-synod-of-bishops-justice-in-the-world-2/.

De Souza, Cyril. "The Process of Inculturation." *Salesianum* 74 (2012) 625–43.

DiGiovanni, Stephen Michael. *Ignatius: The Life of Ignatius Cardinal Kung Pin-Mei*. CreateSpace, 2013.

Dinn, James M. "A Novelist's Miracle: Structure and Myth in *Death Comes for the Archbishop*." *Western American Literature* 7 (1972) 39–46.

Dorschell, Mary Frances. "Mentors and Protégés: Spiritual Evolution in Georges Bernanos' *Under Satan's Sun* and *The Diary of a Country Priest*." *Christianity & Literature* 52 (2002) 3–22.

Ekern, Stener. "The Modernizing Bias of Human Rights: Stories of Mass Killings and Genocide in Central America." *Journal of Genocide Research* 12 (2010) 219–41.

Endo, Shusaku. *Silence*. Tokyo: Sophia University Press, 1969.

Engler, Mark. "Truth and Fantasy." *New Internationalist*, December 2005.

Estrada, Ruth Elizabeth Velasquez. "Grassroots Peacemaking: The Paradox of Reconciliation in El Salvador." *Social Justice* 41 (2015) 69–88.

Finn, James. "Graham Greene as Moralist." *First Things* 3 (1990) 22–29.

Francis, Pope. *Evangelii Gaudium*. https://www.vatican.va/content/francesco/en/apost_exhortations/documents/papa-francesco_esortazione-ap_20131124_evangelii-gaudium.html.

———. *Laudato Si'*. https://www.vatican.va/content/francesco/en/encyclicals/documents/papa-francesco_20150524_enciclica-laudato-si.html.

———. "Message of Pope Francis to the Catholics of China and to the Universal Church." *Tripod* 38 (2018) 68–70.

Gardiner, Anne Barbeau. "The Tears of a Cleric." *New Oxford Review* 82 (2015) 36–40.

Gaston, Georg. *The Pursuit of Salvation: A Critical Guide to the Novels of Graham Greene*. Troy, NY: Whitston, 1984.

Gessel, Van C. "Hearing God in Silence: The Fiction of Endo Shusaku." *Christianity & Literature* 48 (1999) 149–64.

———. "*Silence* on Opposite Shores: Critical Reactions to the Novel in Japan and the West." In *Approaching Silence: New Perspectives on Shusaku Endo's Classic Novel*, edited by Mark W. Dennis and Darren J. N. Middleton, 25–41. London: Bloomsbury Academic, 2015.

"Graham Greene, 86, Dies: Novelist of the Soul." *New York Times*, April 4, 1991, A1, 1.

Greene, Graham. *The Power and the Glory*. New York: Penguin Classics, 2003.

Grogan, Brian. *Pedro Arrupe: A Heart Larger than the World*. Chicago: Loyola, 2022.

Guardado, Ana G. "Outsiders in El Salvador: The Role of an International Truth Commission in a National Transition." *Berkeley La Raza Law Journal* 22 (2012) 433–57.

Gumbleton, Thomas J. "If You Want Peace, Work for Justice." In *Romero's Legacy: The Call to Peace and Justice*, edited by Pilar Hogan Closkey and John P. Hogan, 35–44. Lanham, MD: Rowland & Littlefield, 2007.

Gutiérrez, Gustavo. "Liberation Theology for the Twenty-First Century." In *Romero's Legacy: The Call to Peace and Justice*, edited by Pilar Hogan

Closkey and John P. Hogan, 45–60. Lanham, MD: Rowland & Littlefield, 2007.

Hawley, John C. *Christian Encounters with the Other*. New York: New York University Press, 1998.

Herrera, M. Chris, and Michael G. Nelson. "Salvadoran Reconciliation (El Salvador Armed Forces and Farabundo Marti National Liberation Front)." *Military Review* 88 (2008) 24–30.

Ho, Koon-Ki T. "*Silence* and the Japanization of Christianity." *Japan Christian Quarterly* 53 (1987) 71–76.

"Holding Ourselves Accountable." *National Catholic Reporter* 40 (2004) 28.

Horgan, Paul. "In Search of the Archbishop." *Catholic Historical Review* 46 (1961) 409–27.

Houle, John A. "One of Christ's Heroes." *Homiletic and Pastoral Review* 92 (1992) 58–59.

"How Rome Tried to Censor Greene's Masterpiece." *Guardian*, July 8, 2001. https://www.theguardian.com/uk/2001/jul/08/books.humanities.

Indian Pueblo Cultural Center. "A Brief History of the Pueblo Revolt." https://indianpueblo.org/a-brief-history-of-the-pueblo-revolt/.

"Is Justice Still a Long-Way Off for Jesuit Martyrs in El Salvador?" *America* 222 (2020) 1–3.

Jasper, David. "The Priest in the Novels of Graham Greene." *Theology* 124 (2021) 84–92.

Jin, Luxian. *The Memoirs of Jin Luxian, Volume One: Learning and Relearning 1916–1982*. Hong Kong: Hong Kong University Press, 2012.

John Paul II, Pope. "Chinese Cardinal Ignatius Kung Pin-mei Dies in Stamford, USA." *Catholic Culture*. https://www.catholicculture.org/culture/library/view.cfm?recnum=2634.

———. *Ut Unum Sint*. http://www.vatican.va/content/john-paul-ii/en/encyclicals/documents/hf_jp-ii_enc_25051995_ut-unum-sint.pdf.

Kaethler, Andrew T. J. "I Become a Thousand Men and Yet Remain Myself: Self Love in Joseph Ratzinger and Georges Bernanos." *Logos* 19 (2016) 150–67.

Keegan, John E. "Robert Bresson's *The Diary of a Country Priest*: The Experience of God as Grace." *Sewanee Theological Review* 54 (2010) 47–59.

Keuss, Jeffrey F. "The Lenten Face of Christ in Shusaku Endo's *Silence* and *Life of Jesus*." *Expository Times* 118 (2007) 273–79.

Ladany, Laszlo. *The Catholic Church in China*. New York: Freedom House, 1987.

Lamet, Pedro Miguel. *Pedro Arrupe: Witness of the Twentieth Century, Prophet of the Twenty-First*. Boston: Boston College Institute of Jesuit Sources, 2020.

Leah, Gordon. "A Bad Priest? Reflections on Regeneration in Graham Green's Novel *The Power and the Glory*." *Heythrop Journal* 51 (2010) 18–21.

———. "'Become as a Little Child': Reflections on Georges Bernanos' *Diary of a Country Priest* and Other Works." *Heythrop Journal* 56 (2015) 249–60.

Link, Christopher A. "Bad Priests and the Valor of Pity: Shusaku Endo and Graham Greene on the Paradoxes of Christian Virtue." *Logos* 15 (2012) 75–96.

Lucia, José. "The Anthropological Function of Dialogue in Political Reconciliation Processes." *Ramon Llull Journal of Applied Ethics* 1 (2014) 125–41.

Lye, John. "*The Diary of a Country Priest* and the Christian Novel." *Renascence* 30 (1978) 19–31.

Mariani, Paul Philip. *Church Militant: Bishop Kung and Catholic Resistance in Communist Shanghai.* Cambridge: Harvard University Press, 2011.

———. "The Four Catholic Bishops of Shanghai: 'Underground' and 'Patriotic' Church Competition and Sino-Vatican Relations in Reform-Era China." *Journal of Church and State* 58 (2016) 38–56.

McDermott, Robert T. "In the Footsteps of Martyrs: Lessons from Central America." In *Romero's Legacy: The Call to Peace and Justice*, edited by Pilar Hogan Closkey and John P. Hogan, 15–24. Lanham, MD: Rowman & Littlefield, 2007.

McEntire, Jeffrey L. "Confessions of 'the Weak': The Ecclesiastical Hindrance of Determinism in *Silence*." *Exchange* 49 (2020) 164–78.

McHale, Heather Moreland. "Graham Greene's Pope: Finding God in Battered Places." *America* 213 (2015) 22–24.

Menkhaus, James. "Lessons from the Spirit of Pedro Arrupe: For the Seventieth Anniversary of Hiroshima." *The Way* 55 (2016) 9–19.

Metz, Johannes Baptist, et al. *Martyrdom Today.* Concilium: Religion in the Eighties 163. Edinburgh: T. & T. Clark, 1983.

Minter, Adam. "Keeping Faith." *Atlantic*, July-August 2007. https://www.theatlantic.com/magazine/archive/2007/07/keeping-faith/305990/.

Mong, Ambrose. *Christianity and Western Literature: A Story of Sin and Salvation.* Cambridge: Clarke, 2023.

———. "The Crucified People: Óscar Romero and Martyrdom." *The Way* 60 (2021) 41–56.

———. *Forgiven but Not Forgotten: The Past Is Not Past.* Eugene, OR: Wipf & Stock, 2020.

———. *Sino-Vatican Relations: From Denunciation to Dialogue.* Cambridge: Clarke, 2019.

Netland, John T. "Encountering Christ in Shusaku Endo's Mudswamp of Japan." In *Christian Encounters with the Other*, edited by John C. Hawley, 166–81. New York: New York University Press, 1998.

Okure, Teresa, et al., eds. *Concilium 2003/1: Rethinking Martyrdom.* London: SCM, 2003.

Old, James Paul. "Making Good Americans: The Politics of Willa Cather's *Death Comes for the Archbishop*." *Perspectives on Political Science* 50 (2021) 52–61.

Paul VI, Pope. *Populorum Progressio.* http://www.vatican.va/content/paul-vi/en/encyclicals/documents/hf_p-vi_enc_26031967_populorum.html.

Pellow, C. Kenneth. "The 'Presence' of Dostoevsky in Graham Greene's *The Power and the Glory*." *Renascence* 67 (2015) 57–74.

Peterson, Anna Lisa. *Martyrdom and the Politics of Religion: Progressive Catholicism in El Salvador's Civil War*. Albany, NY: State University of New York Press, 1997.

Peterson, Anna Lisa, and Brandt G. Peterson. "Martyrdom, Sacrifice, and Political Memory in El Salvador." *Social Research* 75 (2008) 511–42.

Pope, Stephen. "The Convergence of Forgiveness and Justice: Lessons from El Salvador." *Theological Studies* 64 (2003) 812–35.

Potts, Matthew Ichihashi. "Christ, Identity, and Empire in *Silence*." *Journal of Religion* 101 (2021) 183–204.

Pryce-Jones, David. *Graham Greene*. Edinburgh: Oliver, 1963.

Rahner, Karl. "Dimensions of Martyrdom: A Plea for the Broadening of a Classical Concept." *Concilium* 163 (1983) 9–11.

———. *Theological Investigations*. Vol. 3. Baltimore: Helicon, 1967.

Sevick, Leona. "Catholic Expansionism and the Politics of Depression in *Death Comes for the Archbishop*." In *The Cambridge Companion to Willa Cather*, edited by Marilee Lindemann, 191–204. Cambridge: Cambridge University Press, 2005.

Shaw, Patrick W. "Women and the Father: Psychosexual Ambiguity in *Death Comes for the Archbishop*." *American Imago* 46 (1989) 61–76.

Silber, Irina Carlota. "Mothers/Fighters/Citizens: Violence and Disillusionment in Post-War El Salvador." *Gender & History* 16 (2004) 561–87.

Sobrino, Jon. *Jesus the Liberator: A Historical Theological Reading of Jesus of Nazareth*. London: Burns & Oates, 1993.

———. "Our World: Cruelty and Compassion." *Concilium* 1 (2003) 15–23.

Spadaro, Antonio. "The Agreement Between China and the Holy See." *La Civiltá Cattolica*, September 25, 2018. https://www.laciviltacattolica.com/the-agreement-between-china-and-the-holy-see/.

St. Amant, Clyde Penrose. "God Gets His Man: A Study of Graham Greene." *Perspectives in Religious Studies* 1 (1974) 55–61.

Teaching Central America. "History of El Salvador." https://www.teachingcentralamerica.org/history-of-el-salvador.

Thiede, John S. *Remembering Oscar Romero and the Martyrs of El Salvador: A Cloud of Witnesses*. Lanham, MD: Lexington, 2017.

"Truth or Consequences in El Salvador: United Nations Truth Commission Human Rights Report." *America* 168 (1993) 3–4.

UCA News. "Bishop Jin of Shanghai Dead at 96." http://www.ucanews.com/news/bishop-jin-of-shanghai-dies-at-97/68064.

Wachal, Christopher B. "Forbidden Ships to Chartered Tours: Endo, Apostasy, and Globalization." In *Approaching Silence: New Perspectives on Shusaku Endo's Classic Novel*, edited by Mark W. Dennis and Darren J. N. Middleton, 91–106. London: Bloomsbury Academic, 2015.

Wang, Zhicheng. "Msgr. Aloysius Jin Luxian, Official Nishop of Shanghai, Has Died." *AsiaNews*, April 27, 2013. http://www.asianews.it/news-en/Msgr.-Aloysius-Jin-Luxian,-official-bishop-of-Shanghai,-has-died-27775.html.

Washburn, Dennis. "Is Abjection a Virtue? Silence and the Trauma of Apostasy." In *Approaching Silence: New Perspectives on Shusaku Endo's Classic Novel*, edited by Mark W. Dennis and Darren J. N. Middleton, 203–21. London: Bloomsbury Academic, 2015.

Watkins, Devin. "Pope Francis Urges Chinese Catholics to Be 'Good Citizens.'" https://www.vaticannews.va/en/pope/news/2023-09/pope-francis-mongolia-china-greetings-mass.html.

Whitehouse, J. C. "'A Certain Idea of Man': The Human Person in the Novels of Georges Bernanos." *Modern Language Review* 80 (1985) 571–85.

"The Witness of Bishop Gong." *America* 153 (1985) 22–23.

# Index